LARGE PRINT

.45-CALIBER DEATHTRAP

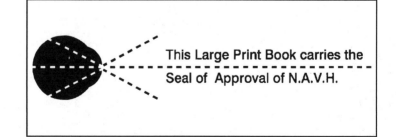

This Large Print Book carries the
Seal of Approval of N.A.V.H.

.45-CALIBER DEATHTRAP

PETER BRANDVOLD

THORNDIKE PRESS
A part of Gale, Cengage Learning

GALE
CENGAGE Learning™

Detroit • New York • San Francisco • New Haven, Conn • Waterville, Maine • London

GALE
CENGAGE Learning

LIBRARY OF CONGRESS CATALOGING-IN-PUBLICATION DATA

Brandvold, Peter.
  .45-caliber deathtrap / by Peter Brandvold.
    p. cm. — (Thorndike Press large print western)
    ISBN-13: 978-1-4104-0693-4 (hardcover : alk. paper)
    ISBN-10: 1-4104-0693-8 (hardcover : alk. paper)
    1. Large type books. I. Title.
  PS3552.R3236A6143 2008
  813'.54—dc22   2008005588

Published in 2008 by arrangement with The Berkley Publishing Group, a member of Penguin Group (USA) Inc.

*To our good friends
and white-water guides
Jan and Sarah
And to their feline gang at the
top of the mountain*

1

Three o'clock in the afternoon of a breezy, sunny autumn day, with a recent snow mantling the high, western peaks of the looming Rockies, Wade Scanlon hoorawed his Murphy freight wagon into the little crossroads town of Columbine Creek, Colorado Territory.

The freighter pulled the mules up before the town's only saloon — a brick-and-adobe hovel with a sod roof and a flower box of dried vines hanging askew beneath the small front window, which sported a bullet hole in its lower right corner, around which finer cracks stretched weblike. A shingle over the brush arbor showed a line sketch of a hog's head, which was the Hog's Head Saloon's only identifying marker.

Scanlon set the brake and blinked against his own dust catching up to him. As the mules drank at one of two stock tanks fronting the saloon's weathered stoop, Scanlon grabbed his canteen, stashed with his rifle beneath the seat, and took a long pull. His throat worked, water streaming from both corners of his broad, mustachioed mouth, before he lowered the hide-covered flask and made a face.

"Christ — warm creek water." He shoved the cork into the mouth and hammered it home with the heel of his hand. "I need a beer!"

Scanlon, who'd lost a leg three years ago to a mountain lion high in the Ramparts, grabbed the cottonwood crutch he'd carved himself, and leapt over the wagon's left front wheel. He hit the ground with the ease of a man accustomed to jumping around on one leg, and deftly set the crutch beneath his right arm.

He hobbled around the back of the wagon, negotiated the two steps to the boardwalk, and yelled through the building's single batwing. "Serenity, you better have some good cold beer in there, or I'm gonna burn your place down!"

"Who's that?" came the nasally voice from within.

Scanlon pushed into the room's dense darkness abuzz with flies and rife with the smell of beer, whiskey, and salt brine. All of the knife-scarred tables were vacant.

"Ah, shit," came the voice from within. "Not you, Scanlon. Anyone but you. I was hopin' you'd run your mules into a canyon!"

The freighter chuckled and bellied up to the bar consisting of two whipsawed pine planks stretched across beer kegs, with a five-gallon jar of pickled hog knuckles adorning the far end. In a matching jar on the right, the Hog's Head owner and operator, Serenity Parker, had pickled a diamondback, eleven feet long and as thick as a fence post. Old Serenity sat in a chair so low behind the bar that Scanlon couldn't see much more than his wizened, gray-bearded face and grimy hat from which his greasy silver hair hung straight to his shoulders. He held a yellowed, quarter-folded newspaper in his knotted, red hands.

"I'm still kickin'. At least, with one leg." Scanlon chuckled at his usual old joke. "Now, what I was sayin' . . ."

"Yeah, I got beer, ye varmint." The old man pushed up from his chair and reached for an overturned beer schooner on the shelf behind him. "But it ain't very cold 'cause I'm outta ice and we've had us a hot spell. So don't go raggin' me about warm beer. You won't find *cold* beer in five hundred square miles less'n you go to Denver to git it, or less'n someone brewin' up on Long's."

9

Scanlon slapped the bar with mock exasperation. "Freighters don't like warm beer, damn ye, Serenity. How many times do I have to tell you? We need the dust cut with somethin' *cold!*"

"There — take it or leave it," Serenity said when he'd drawn the beer and set the foamy mug atop the planks, giving the glass an expert twirl so the handle swung toward Scanlon. Foam licked over the sides to pool around the mug's thick bottom.

"Reckon you leave me no choice," Scanlon said staring down at the beer, savoring it.

"I don't know what you're complainin' about, you one-legged dog. For every three beers you pay for, you drink two on the house."

"On the house, bullshit!" Scanlon objected. "I win those beers fair and square."

"Fair and square, horse plop! You're the only man I know who's low enough to cheat an old man at dice."

Scanlon grinned and took a long sip from the mug, burying his upper lip deep in the snow-white foam. He shook his head and set the mug on the planks. "Ain't cold." He sighed and licked his lips, slitting his eyes. "Warm as mule piss, matter of fact. But dang, if it don't cut the dust."

The oldster stood before Scanlon, his knotted, arthritic fists resting on the bar. "Where you headed?"

"End of the line. The Welcome camp, up on the pass. Cuno got him a contract with a Dutchman plannin' to open a new mercantile . . . soon as we get some freight to him."

"Where is Massey anyways? How come you ain't ridin' together?"

Scanlon sipped his beer and jerked a thumb over his shoulder. "Still waitin' on another load at the rail yard. Only got half the rifles and shovels we ordered. Should be along in a couple days."

"That younker's got sand — I'll say that for young Massey. Openin' up a freight line in this neck of the woods. These mountain trails ain't no easy ride in them heavy wagons. Scalawags around every bend too."

"I'm just grateful fer the job. Hell, before he brought his freight line to Denver, I was emptyin' spittoons at the train depot."

Serenity Parker slapped the bar. "An' even that was too good fer ya!"

Scanlon didn't reply. He'd raised his glass to take a long, heavy pull. Looking over his raised glass, he saw Parker's eyes stray to the dusty front window. A muscle twitched in the old man's haggard face, and one eye slitted warily.

11

Scanlon lowered the mug and followed Serenity's gaze with his own. Several men in rough trail garb were angling toward the saloon from Miss Mundy's whorehouse, which sat beside the livery barn on the other side of the street.

"Ah, shit," the barman exclaimed. "Here they come again."

"Who?" Scanlon asked, watching the tall, bewhiskered riders saunter toward him, their undershot boots puffing up dust in the hay- and manure-flecked street.

"Gang o' hard cases. The scalawags I was just talkin' about. One of 'em's injured, looked like a bullet wound to me. Seen 'em when they first rode in two days ago. They're all holed up at Miss Mundy's, waiting for the bullet-shot hombre to heal. They come over here reg'lar for whiskey, only pay fer half of it."

"Sounds like me," Scanlon said.

"Only they don't even bother to throw dice fer it."

Scanlon and the barman watched through the dust-streaked window as the first two men mounted the boardwalk. The hard cases moved toward the batwing but stopped just outside, raking their gazes across Scanlon's wagon parked before the hitch rack. Ten or so more, all wearing at

12

least one holstered pistol on their hips or in shoulder rigs under their arms, continued filing across the street, their sunburned faces canted toward the team and wagon.

Several voices rose from the boardwalk. One of the men chuckled. Someone commented on the size of the load, while another wondered what the tarp tied over the wagon box was covering.

"Only one way to find out," one of the hard cases drawled.

Scanlon set his near-empty glass down hard and grabbed his crutch. "What the hell they think they're doin'?"

The old apron reached across the bar to grab Scanlon's arm, but missed. "Now, hold on, Wade. Don't be goin' out there. . . ."

Scanlon didn't hear the old bartender's warning. He was shuffling toward the door, the crutch pounding the puncheons as he pushed through the single batwing and stepped onto the boardwalk. He swung his gaze around, rage bubbling in his gut. The dozen or so armed men milled in the street and on the boardwalk, watching a tall, bearded man in a battered leather hat untie one of the four ropes Scanlon had fixed over the wagon's tarp.

The tall man's back faced the saloon. Without turning his head, he said, "Don't

13

just stand there, Hays. Get over to the other side and help me lift this tarp."

"No one lifts that tarp but me or my partner!" Scanlon shouted, outraged. "And you boys can get the hell away from my wagon."

All eyes turned to him, including the tall, bearded gent standing back by the tailgate. He wore a fringed deerskin jacket with Indian beadwork adorning each breast. He wore two .44s on his hips, and another one snugged behind his cartridge belt over his belly.

"Who're you?" the man asked blandly.

"Wade Scanlon. This here's my wagon. Kindly get your hand off that rope."

As Scanlon moved forward, the man to his right kicked the crutch out from beneath Scanlon's right arm. The freighter grunted and fell, rolled off the boardwalk and into the shade that the big Murphy angled over the street.

The hard cases laughed. As Scanlon climbed to his left knee and reached for the crutch, the same hombre who'd tripped him kicked the crutch to the other end of the boardwalk.

"Leave him alone, goddamn ye!" ordered Serenity Parker in his nasal twang, standing just inside the batwing door, his face

14

flushed, eyes pinched with fury.

The man who'd kicked the crutch bolted toward the barman, then stopped short as Serenity scuffled back into the saloon's deep shadows. He turned to the rest of the group, mouth stretched with laughter, sweat sopping his thin blond beard.

"You know who he reminds me of?" asked another hard case — short but lean, with snow-white hair and pink eyes half shaded by his bowler hat. He wore two pearl-butted .45s down low on both hips, and a big, bone-handled bowie was fixed to the top of his right mule-ear boot. "Reminds me of one o' them kangaroos they got down Australia way. A one-legged kangaroo. Sure enough — that's what he is."

Wade Scanlon lay in the dirt beside the boardwalk. He had one arm on the boardwalk, his sole leg curled beneath him. He glanced around at the laughing hard cases and eyed his crutch, feeling helpless as a rabbit in a rattlesnake den. Rage burned in him, turning his features crimson.

"This is my goddamn wagon. Get the hell away, or . . ."

"Or what?" The leader swung the toe of his right boot hard against Scanlon's back. "What's a one-legged kangaroo gonna do about it?"

Seething, clamping his jaws against the pain shooting through his spine, Scanlon craned his neck to stare up at the man. The man nodded to the blond-bearded hombre, then turned to continue loosening the ropes. Soon, they were all jerking and pulling at the ropes, several shucking their bowies or Arkansas toothpicks to hack and saw at the ties holding the canvas in place.

Scanlon lay in the dirt by the right rear wheel, staring up with disbelief as the hard cases tossed away the ropes and jerked the canvas cover off the barrels and crates that Scanlon and Cuno Massey had back-and-bellied and carefully arranged in the Murphy's stout box.

These hyenas meant to rob him blind. What would he tell Cuno?

At the moment, they were too enthralled by the freight to pay him any mind. . . .

While the hard cases jimmied the crates open with their knife blades and gun barrels, whooping and hollering like marauding Apaches, Scanlon hoisted himself onto the boardwalk, then crawled past the saloon door to the boardwalk's far end. He grabbed his crutch, planted the padded end against his armpit, and hoisted himself to his foot.

Inside the saloon, Serenity Parker kept a sawed-off twelve-gauge behind the bar. . . .

Breathing hard through his teeth, Scanlon made for the door.

"Hey, where you goin'?"

Scanlon whipped his head toward the wagon. The hard cases covered the Murphy like buzzards on fresh carrion. A couple were holding up pairs of new denim breeches, as if checking the fit. Another was caressing the barrel of a new Winchester repeater, the smooth walnut stock of which glowed like gold in the angling afternoon light.

The man who'd spoken had a thick, red beard but no mustache and, though a white man, he wore a steeple-crowned sombrero and a bull-hide vest decorated with hammered silver discs. He held a sack of coffee beans in one hand, a can of tomatoes in the other. He glowered down at Scanlon.

The freighter bunched his lips and turned to the door. Before he'd taken a step, a pistol popped. Pain seared Scanlon's knee, and he dropped to the boardwalk.

"Ughhh!"

He looked down. The bullet had hammered into the side of his knee, blood flooding the ragged hole in his pants leg.

Clamping his jaws down tight on the pain, the freighter looked at the wagon. The man in the steeple-brimmed sombrero was still holding the coffee beans. In his other hand, he held a smoking six-shooter. The men around him had stopped looting to regard Scanlon, grinning.

Several pointed and laughed.

"Jesus Christ, Walt," the tall, bearded man exclaimed. "That's the only leg he's got!"

"That's gotta hurt!" whooped another. "Look at him. Why, he's turnin' whiter than this here bakin' powder."

Scanlon clamped both his hands over his shattered knee. Blood gushed through his fingers. His body shook from the pain, as though an Apache war lance had been rammed through the bone.

The ache and the burn chilled him. The boardwalk tipped this way and that, like an unmoored dock.

"Bastards," he grunted. "Sons of thievin', no-good, dirty, soulless whores . . . the lot of ya."

Christ, he'd lost the whole damn load. Over three thousand dollars worth of freight. What would he tell Cuno? What would *they* tell the bank?

He laid his head down against the scarred planks. As the blood drained out his knee, his body weakened, his vision dimmed. Vaguely, as if from far away, he heard the whoops and jubilant yells of the freight

18

thieves. He didn't know how much time had passed when the smell of kerosene filled his nostrils.

He looked at the wagon. They'd turned it around so the mules faced the way Scanlon had come. The bandit leader — the tall, bearded man with three pistols — was shaking kerosene over the near-empty Murphy from one of the large cans Scanlon had been hauling.

"Bastard," Scanlon grunted, not sure if his words carried. "Don't burn my wagon, you bastards."

The gang leader dropped a single match into the bed.

Whoo-oof!

As the inferno grew, the mules kicked and brayed and bolted off down the main drag toward the edge of town. The blazing wagon, a ball of raging fire, bounced along behind. It careened to and fro along the street before it disappeared, leaving a trail of sooty, black smoke in its wake. Behind it, the hard cases coughed and hollered.

There was a shrill scream followed by a ghastly clamor, like distant thunderclaps. Scanlon gnashed his teeth and ground his head against the boardwalk planks, groaning and cursing.

The mules had run off the road and into

the gorge northwest of town.

He slitted his tear-glazed eyes as he returned his gaze to the street.

In front of the saloon, two hard cases danced arm-in-arm, laughing. One wore a new fur cap and fur mittens while the other had donned a woman's torn gingham dress and a poke bonnet. The others were still going through the crates and barrels they'd tossed from the wagon. A couple were shoving each other and cursing.

In his mind's eye, Scanlon saw Serenity Parker's sawed-off gut shredder.

He threw out his bloody right hand, reaching under the door, digging his fingers between puncheons for purchase. Before he could crawl more than three feet, someone grabbed his ankle and pulled him back onto the boardwalk.

Scanlon felt as though an ax had been driven through his knee. The freighter screamed.

The bandit leader crouched over him, shaking his head. A red-throated hummingbird had been tattooed into the man's right cheek, above his scraggly black beard and just below his blind, milky eye. His misshapen nose was broad as a wedge.

"What am I gonna do with you, kangaroo-man?"

Scanlon cursed and spat in the man's face.

The man only grinned and raised one of his three pistols. He extended the barrel at Scanlon's head.

The freighter grimaced. Not so much for himself. He'd let down the only man who'd offered him a decent stake since he'd lost his leg.

Cannady's index finger drew taut against the trigger.

The hammer snapped down.

Scanlon didn't feel a thing.

2

Sitting the driver's box of his big Murphy freight wagon — a platform-spring dray, with a high seat and chains from axle to double-tree for sharp cornering — Cuno Massey poked his flat-brimmed Stetson off his forehead and loosened his neckerchief.

His second day on the trail, he was fifty miles northwest of Denver. He and his two stocky mules rode straight through the heart of desolate nowhere — into the foothills and sandstone scarps of the Rocky Mountain's Front Range, with only rabbitbrush, sage, occasional cottonwoods, and autumn flocks of raucous blackbirds for company.

A warm wind blew over the high, western peaks, bringing the smell of sage and dry sand and . . . coffee.

He sniffed the wind.

Sure enough.

Someone was brewing a pot of good six-shooter mud not far to the south. The worry lines in Cuno's blond brow softened. He'd probably just found his partner, Wade Scanlon, with whom Cuno had opened a freight business a year ago this December. Actually, it was Cuno's father's old business. Cuno had bought it back from the man he'd sold it to when he'd gone after the two men who'd raped and murdered his stepmother before killing his father as well. Cuno had then moved the business from Nebraska to Denver, to shuttle freight between Denver and the gold camps dotting the Front Range.

Wade Scanlon was two days late getting back to town after the load of dry goods and rifles he'd hauled to the new settlement along Sunburst Creek. Cuno had feared Wade had run into Southern Cheyenne, known to be on the prowl in this neck of the rimrocks.

The coffee could indeed be Wade's. The only thing Wade enjoyed more than coffee was beer.

Cuno plucked his Winchester repeater off the wagon seat, jacked a shell into the chamber, off-cocked the hammer, and laid the rifle across his knees. He removed his right glove in case he needed that hand for shooting. He steered the wagon off the road and stared expectantly over the mules' bob-

23

bing heads as he crested a low rise and started down the other side.

At the bottom of the hill, in a fold between fall-brown hogbacks, two men sat around a wind-battered fire, slumped deep in their patched wool coats, steaming tin cups in their hands. Their collars were pulled up, their hats pulled down over their eyes. One wore a muffler over his hat, tied beneath his chin.

Both looked up, frowning as the big wagon rolled toward them behind the lumbering mules, whose breath rose and tore on the wind. Neither of the men was Wade Scanlon, and Wade's Murphy was nowhere in sight.

Damn.

Balancing his rifle across his knees, Cuno hauled back on the reins. "Whoo-ahh. Whoah, now."

One of the two men around the fire gained his feet. The other man, whose long, salt-and-pepper hair fell to his shoulders, remained where he was. A Spencer .56 leaned against the log beside him. He squinted at Cuno, carving deep lines around his eyes and down both sides of his long, thin nose.

The mules stopped. Sensing no danger here, Cuno left the rifle where it was, holding the ribbons but ready to drop them if his instincts proved wrong.

He raised his voice to be heard against the wind and crackling fire. "Howdy."

The older man remained squatting, expressionless. The younger, standing man nodded, offering a cordial "How-do."

"A little chilly today."

"A mite," said the squatting man. He looked Cuno over closely, then glanced at the charred pot resting on a flat rock in the fire. "We have some coffee here. You're welcome to a cup."

Cuno didn't want coffee just yet. He'd intended to make it to Columbine Creek before full dark. But it was impolite to turn down the offer, and he couldn't ask about Wade until he partook of the pilgrims' generosity. He gave them another quick glance. Probably a couple of market hunters or saddle tramps riding the winter grub-line, heading south toward warmer weather.

Cuno set the wagon's brake, left his rifle on the wagon seat, and climbed down. He rummaged around in the wagon box for a cup, then walked over, squatted down, and filled the cup. He blew on the hot liquid, sipped. He had to swallow twice to keep it down.

"That's good." Cuno cleared his throat. What had they made this stuff out of —

25

mule shit? "Damn good."

"Billy made it," the younger man said.

The older gent flushed slightly as he stared at the flames. "Trick is to add a little eatin' tobaccy and sugar to the grounds. Just a pinch of black powder." Without pausing, he added, "I'm Billy Hopgood, and that's Delvin Squires. We're headed down Texas way." They were both too shy and backward to shake hands, so Cuno didn't attempt the gesture either.

"We're cousins," Squires said, chuckling as if it were a joke between them.

"Our daddies were cousins," Billy said. "But hell, I'm old enough to be the kid's uncle. And I have to act that way half the time, or Delvin'd find himself up shit creek without a bull boat!"

He laughed. Delvin bit his lower lip and flushed. He poked a stick at the fire, stirring the ashes around the pot. So quickly as to be nearly imperceptible, his eyes flicked over Cuno's right shoulder, brushing the mules and wagon behind him, canvas stretched over the high side panels on the outside of which hung feed bags, a pick and shovel, an iron wedge, and a jack. Just as quickly, the small, gray-blue eyes slid conspiratorially toward the older man before returning to the stick with which he stirred the ashes.

26

Cuno pretended not to notice. He introduced himself, told the two men he was taking his freight load to Welcome, and asked if they'd seen his partner anywhere along the road. "Big, friendly man in a blue coat. Would have been driving a wagon like mine."

Billy and Delvin said they hadn't seen him.

Cuno finished the putrid coffee as fast as he could without throwing up. He tossed the grounds into the fire.

"You'll be headin' out then?" Billy said.

"Better get back on the trail."

Billy's eyes flicked to his partner, cunning burning in them like a slow-building fire. When they turned to Cuno, they looked distracted. While Billy kept a neutral expression on his face, his shoulders grew taut.

Cuno looked at him directly. "Don't do it, Billy. My rifle's in the wagon, but I've got two forty-fives under this coat." Cuno switched his gaze to Delvin. "My coat's buttoned, but I'll guaran-damn-tee you that I can reach my pistols before you can aim those rifles."

Flushing, Billy furrowed his brows, slitted his eyes, and pooched out his lips. His eyes rolled toward Delvin, who had slipped his hand halfway into his coat.

"Show me that hand," Cuno told him mildly.

Dropping his gaze with chagrin, Delvin slid his hand out of his coat.

"Button up."

"Ah, hellkatoot!" Delvin complained.

When he'd buttoned the two buttons he'd opened while he'd thought the freighter had been obliviously sipping his coffee, Cuno rose and backed toward his mules. His instincts hadn't failed him. Billy and Delvin were harmless enough. They were also down-at-heel enough that staring across the fire at Cuno's wagon, mounted with valuable freight, they'd acquired dangerous ideas. They hadn't seen Wade, but even if they had, Wade, who'd been a deputy sheriff as well as a shotgun rider for a stage line, could have handled these two with ease.

"Hey," Billy said as Cuno climbed up to his seat. "You said your name was Cuno?"

"That's right."

"Shit." Billy looked at Delvin, still hanging his head in shame. "He's the younker that took down those two hide hunters that killed his parents. What were their names? Spoon and . . . and . . ."

Cuno slipped the reins from the brake handle and released the brake with a single chop of his left hand. "Sammy Spoon and

28

Rolf Anderson."

Delvin raised his eyes, more closely scrutinizing Cuno's husky, muscular frame, the wheat-blond hair falling from the young freighter's slouch hat to brush his broad shoulders. "Damn, that was you?"

"That's right."

"How'd you kill those two varmints anyways?" asked Billy.

"I shot Spoon through the brisket as he charged me on horseback," Cuno said, adjusting the reins in his hands. "Beat the hell out of Anderson, drove his own knife through his head."

Billy and Delvin stared over the fire at him, their jaws sagging, apprehension and admiration narrowing their eyes.

Cuno backed the team away from the fire. Over the mules' heads, he regarded the grub-liners with pinched eyes and a heavy jaw, trying to look as crazy as the bounty hunter, Ruben Pacheca, who too had once fogged his trail, before Cuno had killed him.

"I didn't leave either one with very nice-lookin' corpses." Cuno wrinkled his nose. "After I cut their heads off and gouged out their eyes, I cut out their livers and ate 'em both raw." He stopped the team, turned it back toward the trail, and glanced over his shoulder at the two men regarding him

29

warily. "Developed kind of a taste for man liver."

He turned forward, flicked the reins over the mules' backs, and headed back over the rise.

Owl-eyed, Delvin turned to Billy. "Shee-it."

Driving deeper into the foothills, Cuno meandered through the hogbacks and river bottoms. He saw no sign of Wade. It wasn't possible that he could have missed his partner. While the country was crisscrossed with old Indian traces and stock trails, there was only one main wagon trail curving around the camelbacks and rimrocks dividing the mountains from the prairie.

Late in the day, with shadows tilting out from the vaulting western ridges, Cuno approached Columbine Creek, the roofs of the livery barn and saloon rising above the bunchgrass tufts and sage. He turned to look into the ravine opening right of the trail, then hauled back on the reins, planting both boots against the dashboard and yelling, "Whooooo-ah! Hold up there, boys."

He stared into the ravine, twenty feet deep by thirty feet wide. Piled up at the base of the opposite side lay the charred and broken wreckage of a wagon. The wagon lay atop the charred, broken carcasses of two heavy horses or mules.

It looked as though the wagon had tried to leap the ravine but hadn't made it.

But no wagon master — not even a *drunk* wagon master — would try such a fool stunt, even with a wagon as empty as that one had been.

But Cuno knew the wagon hadn't tried to leap the ravine. His mind was only trying to busy itself, spinning in circles, avoiding what Cuno knew in his heart was true.

He set the brake, hit the dirt with both heels, and scrambled down the ravine. Breathing hard, he hunkered down beside the burned-out hulk, wincing against the stench of the charred, rotting mule carcasses.

The hide was so badly burned that he couldn't tell the color of either mule, but he saw the brand burned into one — the brand of the man from whom he'd purchased the beast. The wagon owned the heavy chassis and stocky, high-walled box of a Murphy.

No sign of Wade. That didn't mean he wasn't here. He could be under the mules or under the wagon, burned to fine ashes.

Where was the freight?

Cuno stood and made a reconnaissance,

tramping up and down the ravine for a half mile in each direction. Finding no sign of Wade, he scrambled back up to his wagon, threw the brake, and flicked the ribbons over the team.

Riding with his jaws set hard, he raked his eyes along both sides of the trail. The wagon rounded a slow bend and cleaved the little town of Columbine, the livery barn and whorehouse appearing on his left, the Hog's Head Saloon shoving up on his right.

Scanlon was known to frequent the whorehouse on occasion, but he'd have had a beer first with Serenity Parker.

Cuno stopped the wagon near the three saddle horses tied to the hitch rack in front of the Hog's Head. He remained seated, staring around the street at the several empty crates and barrels littering the street near the saloon, several overturned or broken, their lids tossed about like a child's discarded toys.

He climbed down, glanced at the horses, mounted the boardwalk, and pushed through the hovel's single batwing.

The old man's gray-bearded visage hovered over the bar.

"Serenity, you seen Wade?"

The old man's face bleached. His eyes grew sharp and tense as he glanced over the bar at the three men lounging around the table to Cuno's left. Two sat with their backs to the wall, one arm on the table, near shot glasses and beer schooners. Their rheumy eyes regarded Cuno with casual insolence. The third man faced the wall, elbows on the table. He craned his neck to peer around his chair back, coolly taking Cuno's measure.

They were all armed with pistols. Two rifles leaned against the wall nearby.

Serenity Parker sputtered and stammered. "C-come on back here. There's somethin' I want you to see."

He ambled down the bar and into the room's rear shadows. Cuno tossed another glance at the three men to his left, then followed Serenity to the back and out the rear door.

There was a stable out back, near a thin neck of the same ravine in which Cuno had found the wagon. He followed the oldster inside and stared down at a hand-hewn coffin resting on a rusty wheelbarrow. Fresh sawdust and shavings told Cuno the coffin had been built recently. Yesterday or even today.

Muttering and wheezing, tears rolling down his cheeks, Serenity lifted the coffin lid. A shaft of sunlight angling through the barn's single window shone in the half-open eyes of Wade Scanlon. The freighter lay with his hands crossed on his belly, shoulders crowded by the too-small coffin, head canted slightly to one side.

A small, round hole lay in the dead center of his forehead.

The breeches around his only knee were blood-caked.

His lips were slightly twisted, as if the freighter, known for practical jokes and other such high jinks, was stifling a laugh. His straight, brown hair was neatly combed with pomade.

Cuno stared down at his partner for a long time. His fists were clenched.

While he stared, Serenity Parker told him what happened. The old man paused several times to blow his nose with a grimy red handkerchief.

"I didn't do nothin'," the oldster confessed, his voice breaking. "I just stood there like a dumb old dog. Didn't even go for my shotgun. Couldn't move my damn feet."

Cuno said nothing. He stared at the hole in Wade's forehead.

"My nerves," said Serenity, "they been all shot to hell ever since that dynamite blast in the mine."

"Where'd they go?" Cuno asked.

Serenity shuffled around to peer up from Cuno's left shoulder. "Those three inside are part of the same bunch. They're stayin' with the injured hombre while the rest — ten men if there was one — rode up trail. They're headed to pull a robbery on the western slopes, I heard tell. Probably in Sundance. They're on the dodge. One of the girls from the pleasure house said they robbed a bank out Nebraska way!"

Cuno turned.

"What're you gonna do?" Serenity asked as Cuno left the stable.

"You stay here," the freighter said. "I'll be back to bury my partner."

He crossed the alley and pushed through the Hog's Head's rear door, swinging his gaze around. The three hard cases were no longer in the building. Their voices rose from outside. They were moving around on the street in front of the dusty window.

"Damn, looky here!" one bellowed. "Chewin' tobacco!"

Cuno moved to the front door. Staring out, he removed the keeper thong from over the hammer of his .45.

The three hard cases had the tarp half off the big Murphy, and one was prying the lid off a crate.

3

Cuno slid the Colt from its holster, crouched, and triggered three quick shots. One after another, the hard cases' hats were ripped from their heads to sail around on the breeze before bouncing off along the street.

Each man jerked with alarm, turned enraged looks at the brawny freighter, who held his smoking .45 on the saloon's front boardwalk. He regarded each man mildly.

"I don't know what you're lookin' for, but that's my freight. Less'n you don't stand clear, my next shot's gonna be a mite lower."

They stared at him hard, their hands slowly moving toward the six-shooters holstered low on their thighs.

Cuno's Colt roared again. The man standing at the wagon's tailgate, a wad of fresh chew balling his cheek, crumpled, screaming and clutching his knee. "I apologize," said Cuno. "I must not have made myself clear."

While the wounded man dropped lower into the dusty street, groaning and spitting curses, the others raised their hands high above their pistol butts.

"Hold on, hold on," said the hard case standing atop a crate of winter mackinaws, his long, stringy black hair blowing in the breeze. "We heard you. We just thought this stuff was for sale is all."

"Yeah, don't get your back up," said the other man, kneeling atop flour sacks stacked as high as the Murphy's yellow-painted driver's seat. "We were fixin' to pay."

He wore a denim jacket over a torn underwear shirt and an Abe Lincoln stovepipe hat, a deck of cards wedged behind its braided leather band. The breeze buffeted the fringes of his deerskin leggings.

Cuno gritted his teeth and jerked his .45's hammer back with an angry rasp. "Ain't for sale. Get down."

"All right," said the man with the stringy black hair, glancing at the man in the stovepipe hat.

He shrugged, crouched, planted both hands on the side of the wagon box, and hoisted himself over. He dropped with a thud, dust puffing around his worn boots. A second later, the other man joined him, catching his hat as it tumbled off his shoulder.

The other man lay at the back of the wagon, both legs curled beneath his body. He clutched his bloody knee with his right hand. His face, framed by two dusty wings of sandy-blond hair, was nearly as red as the blood streaming between his fingers.

"You son of a bitch," he spat at Cuno. "You ruined my goddamn knee!"

"Shut up," Cuno said, "or I'll ruin the other one."

He stared at the other two, who'd stepped out of the wagon's purple shade, casually putting a good six feet between them. They kept their hands well above their pistol butts, but sneers flashed in their eyes and pulled at their lips.

"You sure are proddy," said Stovepipe, grinning.

"We told ya we was fixin' to pay," said the man beside him. "Just wanted to see if ya had anything worth payin' *for.*" He shrugged and canted his head to one side, flashed a toothy smile.

"That what you told Wade Scanlon?"

The two men looked at each other.

"Now, who's that?" Stovepipe asked.

"The one you shot in the knee and right

here." Cuno put a finger to his forehead. His cheeks were taut, forked veins swelling just above the bridge of his nose. "Before you looted his wagon, set it on fire, and hoorawed his team into the ravine back yonder."

"Oh, kangaroo-man!" said the man with the stringy black hair. "Jeez, I plum forgot about him."

"How could you forgit him?" said Stovepipe, laughing. "Don't you remember, Walt shot him in the knee just like this bastard shot Cotton over yonder. Only, that was the only knee kangaroo-man had!"

They laughed.

"And Cannady shot Wade between his eyes!" Stovepipe added.

They laughed again.

"Where might I find this Cannady?" Cuno asked.

"Oh," Stringy Hair said, "you don't wanna find Cannady. He's off his feed. He done had to leave his injured brother with the whores. Besides, he's faster'n downwind spit, an' mean as a rattlesnake in a fryin' pan."

Stovepipe's eyes flicked toward the wounded man behind the wagon. Cuno swung left. His Colt barked at the same time the S&W of the knee-shot man burned a round through Cuno's left calf. Cuno's slug

39

smashed the wounded man's head straight back in the street, its quarter-sized hole leaking blood.

In the corner of his right eye, Cuno saw the other two hard cases reach for their guns. He dove forward as the pistols popped, drilling the air where he'd been standing, the slugs plunking into the saloon and the awning posts behind him.

He hit the dirt behind the wagon and scrambled to a crouch as two more shots plunked into the wagon box, spraying his face with wood slivers. He snaked his Colt around the wagon's right rear corner. The two hard cases were sidestepping toward the saloon but facing the wagon, crouched, pistols extended, trying to get a bead on their quarry.

Cuno triggered one shot, then another, watched as both men fired their own revolvers into the dirt and went down, screaming. Raging, bleeding from his lower left shoulder, Stovepipe swung his revolver toward the wagon and sparked a round off a small iron tie ring right of Cuno's face.

Gritting his teeth, Cuno drilled two rounds into the man's chest.

As Stovepipe wailed, kicking around in the dust like an overheated horse, Stringy Hair ran heavy-footed, right hand held tight to his wounded hip, around the far side of the saloon. Cuno stood and opened his Colt's loading gate. As he shook out the spent shells and replaced them with fresh ones, the saloon's single door squawked.

Serenity Parker stepped out, looking around warily.

"Stay inside, Serenity." Cuno flipped the loading gate closed. "Got a little moppin' up to do."

Parker made a hasty retreat, the door swinging shut behind him.

As Cuno moved to the saloon's corner, following Stringy Hair's scuffling tracks, he saw that several scantily clad women had moved out of the whorehouse and into the street, looking around wide-eyed. Several others remained on the unpainted house's sagging front porch.

"Lara, get back here!" one called to a girl moving toward the wagon. "You wanna get *shot?*"

Cuno waved the women back and tramped along the saloon's west wall, following blood splashed in the gravel and rabbitbrush around the saloon's rear corner to the backyard.

Ca-pop! Zing!

As the slug sliced off a rock near Cuno's left boot, the shooter ran out from behind

41

an old beer barrel, heading for the barn. Crouching, Cuno fired two quick shots. The man screamed and fell inside the barn, scrambled back behind the door.

His Colt appeared around the door, just below the hide-loop handle. It barked twice, the barrel belching smoke and stabbing flames.

The man pulled the gun back.

Cuno aimed his .45 at the door and emptied it, the four slugs tracing a circle the size of a coffee lid.

There was a wooden thud. The door jerked. Stringy Hair's head appeared, sagging slowly down to the hay-flecked ground beside the door. The open eyes did not blink. Blood washed over his lips and down his chin, dribbled into the dust.

The saloon's back door scraped open. In the crack, the old bartender's face appeared, owl-eyed. When soft footfalls sounded behind Cuno, he spun, extending his empty gun. A girl. She flinched, took one step back.

"There's another one in the house," she said.

It was Lara, with soft yellow hair and sandstone-colored eyes, a mole on her right cheekbone, another just above her nose. The blemishes did nothing to mar her beauty. Cuno had wondered what had turned such a sweet, pretty girl to whoring until she'd told him, the last time he was through Columbine, that her parents had broken up and simply abandoned her on the streets of Denver.

That was often all it took.

Cuno swung past her, looked at the house. In the second story, a lace curtain swung down across a window.

"Wounded?"

"Yeah, but he's getting better," Lara said. "He's also got one of them big, long pistols. Near as long as a rifle."

"A Buntline Special," Cuno said, thumbing fresh cartridges through his loading gate.

"He's got a taste for strange pleasures too."

"Not much longer."

Cuno tramped with her toward the house, behind which the sun was setting, casting shadows into the yard around half a dozen half-dressed girls.

"Sorry about what happened to Scanlon," Lara said gently behind him.

"Stay here."

Holding his .45 down low at his right thigh, Cuno passed the girls standing silent amidst the buckbrush and sage of the pleasure house's front yard. As he climbed the porch and started through the open front door, a plump, middle-aged woman with bottle-blond hair piled loosely atop her head grabbed his left arm.

"He was upstairs beatin' hell outta one of my girls a while ago. Haven't heard a peep out of him since the shootin' started." Her breath smelled like candy and tobacco, Miss Mundy's two worst vices. She read the Bible aloud to her girls every Sunday, however, and did not personally imbibe.

Cuno nodded and moved slowly through the door. He crossed the shabby parlor to the stairs and the room's rear, took the carpeted stairs two steps at a time, walking softly on the balls of his boots, the .45 aimed straight out from his right side.

He gained the top step and stopped.

The air was rife with the smell of whiskey, tobacco, perfume, and sex. A window at the far end of the hall offered the only light.

Cuno took one step forward. A latch clicked. A door on his right and ten yards ahead swung inward. Soft, natural light spread across the hall's musty runner and opposite wall. A bulky shadow grew on the wallpaper.

A skinny, naked man stepped into the hall and turned to face Cuno. He held a naked girl before him, one hand clutching her arm, the other holding a long-barreled pistol to

44

her head.

The man wasn't much taller than the girl, and he wasn't much broader. His blond hair was longer than hers, reaching nearly to his waist. His left side was covered with a heavy, white bandage crisscrossed with cotton straps. His face was long and narrow, his eyes blinking rapidly.

Cuno heard his short, shallow breaths. The girl groaned softly, her body rigid with fear. The fetor of the ground roots, mud, horse shit, and whiskey packing the man's gunshot wound instantly overcame all the other smells in the hall.

The hard case gave the girl's hair a vicious yank. "Throw the gun down, you murderin' bastard! I'll kill the whore!"

Cuno stopped and lowered the gun to his side. "What do I care about a whore?" he asked quietly.

"I'll kill her!" the hard case shrieked. "I swear I will. You'll have this whore's death on your conscience for the rest of your life." He jerked the girl's head sharply; she screamed.

"No," she whimpered, grabbing at the man's skinny arm wrapped around her neck. "Please . . ."

Cuno blinked. "What's your name, friend?"

The hard case stared at him dully, the bridge of his nose wrinkling. "Huh?"

"What's your name?"

"Sylvester. Sylvester Cannady. Why you askin'?"

"Just wanna know what name to carve on your headstone."

As the hard case's mouth snapped wide with exasperation, Cuno raised his pistol and fired. In the close quarters, the report sounded like a shotgun's boom. Smoke wafted as the hard case flew straight back, hitting the floor with an ear-ringing roar. The entire floor jumped and, farther down the hall, a glass chimney shattered as it fell from a bracket lamp.

The girl screamed and bolted to the wall to Cuno's right. She dropped to her butt, brought her knees to her chest, her hands to her face.

"He's crazy!" she shrieked. "He's just plumb *crazy!*"

Cuno walked past her, stared down at the hard case. The man's mouth was still open, flooded with blood from the bullet Cuno had fired between his open jaws. His eyes flickered at the ceiling before a gray veil closed down.

"Not anymore he ain't," Cuno said.

Hurried footsteps rose behind him. Cuno

turned to see Lara running up the stairs, holding her skirts above her ankles. She flashed Cuno a worried look as she went to the whore in the hall.

Cuno holstered his pistol, grabbed the naked hard case's ankles, and pulled him down the stairs, the man's bloody head bouncing with dull thuds.

4

Blacky Gilman, owner and operator of Blacky's Place in Spinoff Creek, twenty miles west of Columbine, looked around his dingy saloon, where four bearded men sat drinking and playing cards, and cursed. He rubbed his hands on his beer-spattered apron and walked out from behind his plank bar to the saloon's back door.

He poked his head out.

"Goddamnit, Chinaman, get in here and put some food on. I'm gonna have miners in here in a half hour, and if they don't get vittles from me, they're gonna head on up the road and get 'em from Gault. God*damn* your lazy, yella hide!"

Gilman cursed again, smoothed a stray lock of frizzy, colorless hair over his bald, bullet-shaped head, and let the door slap shut. His enormous gut bouncing and straining his leather galluses, he ambled back behind the bar and continued stocking his shelves with whiskey bottles from a wooden crate.

He'd arranged two more bottles when the back door creaked open and a slightly built Chinaman in overlarge denim trousers and a gray wool shirt shuffled into the long, narrow room with an armload of stove wood. Rawhide galluses held his pants on his skinny hips. His thinning, black hair was combed straight back from his domed forehead, and a thin growth of beard hung from his chin, something between a goatee and a beard. His feet were clad in beaded Indian moccasins.

"I must split wood, Mr. Geelman. The kid, he no split wood this morning. I must split for myself. That is why I slow with supper vittles. I hurry now, though."

The barman snorted caustically. "The kid took sick. So you have to split wood as well as cook. My heart bleeds for you." Gilman turned his sweaty face to the Chinaman, who was piling wood in the box beside the big brick fireplace along the far wall. "Where's your girl?"

"She clean fish — Li Mei. Clean fish for constable. You know how he like his trout for supper!"

"Forget the fish. Fetch her in here to start servin' drinks. If she's too slow again tonight, I'm gonna hang a price around her neck and let the boys take her into the back room for a little slap 'n' tickle."

Several chuckles rang out from the table near the room's front. The Chinaman, Kong Zhao, dropped a log in the wood box and turned his glance toward the bar, scowling at his boss's back. He clenched his fists, then planted a hand on his right thigh, pushed himself to his feet, and shuffled over to the door.

"I get her now, Boss," he said in his practiced, kowtowing English, bobbing his head. "I get Li Mei right 'way!"

He pushed the back door open, swung his gaze around the saloon's small backyard to the diminutive Chinese girl cleaning fish at a low work bench. Gutted brook trout lay in a slimy pile to one side of the bench, glistening in the early evening light angling over the canyon's tall ridges. Beside the girl's split-log chair was a wooden bucket partly filled with livery-colored fish guts.

Kong Zhao spoke several commanding words of Chinese. The girl set her knife down beside the fish she'd been cleaning, dipped her hands in a pan of water, and shuffled toward the saloon. She gazed fearfully up at her father, who stepped aside to let her pass through the door.

As she stepped over the threshold, he grabbed her slender arm. She swung toward him, her delicate face turned up toward his, her brown eyes questioning.

He muttered a question.

She nodded and, glancing warily about the saloon, turned back to her father. She pinched up the left leg of her baggy denim trousers. In a soft leather sheath strapped about her ankle lay a thin, silver-trimmed, ivory-handled stiletto.

Kong Zhao nodded and released the girl's arm. She walked past her father, tense as always when entering the saloon, and headed for the bar where Gilman was setting freshly filled beer mugs on a wooden tray.

At the same time, the gang of riders led by Clayton Cannady, who'd dubbed themselves "The Committee" during a night of heavy drinking, galloped along the narrow wagon road twisting along the south bank of Chicken Hawk Creek. They were eleven riders — hard, dusty men in various style of ratty dress, with six-guns on their hips, knives in their boots or sheathed between their shoulder blades, rifles in their saddle boots.

As distinctly as each was dressed and

armed, there was one thing they all had in common — each had the reputation for being "touched."

Loco as a peach orchard sow and deadlier than the Devil on a Saturday night.

Each one had killed more times than he could count on both hands. Each man had a bounty on his head, but very few bounty hunters, let alone bona fide badge toters, valued their lives so little as to fog the gang's trail. U.S. marshals had been known, when spying more than one or two members of the gang in one place, to turn around and walk the other way.

"Hey, Cannady," said Ned Crockett, riding off the outlaw leader's right stirrup. He jerked a nod at the wooden sign marking an intersecting trail just ahead and closing. "What say we head on over to Blacky's Place in Spinoff Creek and get us a drink?"

The outlaw leader frowned and checked his horse down to a trot. "Blacky's Place?"

"It's a little dive this fat bastard from Arkansas put up along Spinoff Creek. Last time I was through, it was the only wooden building in town."

"Don't got time for side trips," Cannady growled.

"It's only two miles," said the small, half-Mex child killer named Waco, riding just behind Cannady. "I was through there just last month. Good whiskey. And the trail circles around that mountain, leads back to the main trail ahead. Wouldn't be like we'd be backtrackin' or nothin'."

Cannady reined his horse to a halt, swept dust from the hummingbird tattoo beneath his blind left eye. "Do I need to remind you boys we got us a bank to rob?"

"Not for four days," said Ed Brown, the only black man in the bunch. Six feet four and nearly three hundred pounds, he'd long ago discovered that only a hefty mule could carry his gargantuan carcass for any distance over a mile. He was clad in smelly deerskins and wore a leather, narrow-billed immigrant cap. A heavy Sharps rifle hung by a leather lanyard down his broad back.

"We can make it to Sundance in three days easy," said Ned Crockett, puffing the quirley so perpetually wedged in one corner of his mouth that it had carved its own black furrow in his lips. "What's the hurry?"

"Yeah, what's the hurry?" said Young Knife, the only full-blood Indian, a Ute, in the bunch. "Me, I'm thirsty!"

Cannady looked around at the rocky ridges lining the trail, then glanced at the wooden arrow pointing south along a shaggy two-track wagon trace. "If you boozers need a drink so goddamn bad, then I reckon we'd best get you one. But only *one.* I don't like side trips!"

Later, as the group trotted their horses through a small canyon carved by Spinoff Creek, Ned Crockett turned to Cannady riding to his left. "What's eatin' you, Boss? Is it Sylvester?"

Cannady turned his head to spit tobacco juice over his left stirrup. Running the back of his gloved hand across his mouth, he shrugged. "Sylvester don't do well on his own. Never has. Hell, I had to bottle-feed the whelp till he was eighteen years old. I swear, he'd never have eaten a damn thing, and he'd have left the house without his gun or bowie knife." Cannady plucked a tobacco braid from his shirt pocket and eyed it thoughtfully. "You know how he is. Hell, he's even crazier than I am. Takes after our ma's side."

"You left three good men with him, Clayton. He'll be all right. Hell, they'll probably start out tomorrow and catch up to us in time for the holdup on Tuesday."

"We left three men who I thought could feed and clothe my little brother and tend his wound," Cannady said. "None of 'em can shoot worth shit, if it comes to that. Rodeo — he's good in a knife fight — but I

54

only brought him into the group 'cause he's Waco's cousin, and I owed Waco a favor."

Crockett scowled at the gang leader, smoke puffing out the side of his mouth not holding the cigarette. "Clayton, you're just a damn worrywart, you know that?"

Because he and Cannady had both left Missouri together just after the War, Crockett was the only man in the bunch who could rib the outlaw leader without getting carved up like a Thanksgiving turkey, or having the barrel of a six-gun shoved up his ass and fired.

"Shit," Cannady said, cracking a sheepish smile. "You're right, Ned. I think too much, and that leads to worry. I'm with the savage — let's get a drink!"

He gave a rebel whoop and gigged his zebra dun into a gallop, the rest of the gang following suit. They didn't gallop far before the little tent town of Spinoff Creek appeared around a bend in the trail — a dozen or so dirty white tents, a mud-and-brick livery stable with two peeled-log corrals and a windmill, and a two-story saloon with a broad front porch.

The saloon looked like something out of Cheyenne or Denver. No question it had been built by a man with full confidence in Spinoff Creek's booming prospects. The dull green paint peeling off the sun-blistered boards, however, and the lack of other significant buildings surrounding it, attested to the builder's chagrin.

The gang tied their horses where other horses were tied at the two hitch racks and, slapping their hats against their thighs and raising a miniature dust storm along the shaggy main drag, mounted the porch and split the batwings to enter the saloon.

The Chinaman, Kong Zhao, had just walked out of the saloon's back kitchen, carrying a heavy iron pot with two thick wedges of leather, when the batwing doors creaked and spurs chinged loudly across the puncheons. He paused halfway to the fireplace, and swung his gaze toward the front of the smoky, low-ceilinged room.

Men filed in. Hard-faced riders, well-armed, with the looks of seasoned killers about their sharp eyes and craggy faces. After seven years on the American frontier, raising a young daughter, Kong could smell the evil of such men from a long way off.

The newcomers, boots pounding and spurs singing, dropped into chairs or lined out along the bar. Kong snapped his gaze to his daughter. Head bowed, jet-black hair hiding her face, Li Mei arranged beer mugs on the wooden tray at the bar.

"Beers for my boys!" intoned one of the hard cases, pounding both fists on the bar planks. "And shots all around. For the good gentlemen over there as well," he added with a nod to the four bearded prospectors, who'd recently come in from their diggings.

The miners nodded; one raised his near-empty beer mug in salute.

While the hard cases talked in their harsh, ebullient tones, lighting cigarettes or cigars, coins clanging on the bar top and a deck of cards being riffled, Kong Zhao hung his stew kettle over the fire. He cast dark, furtive looks at the newcomers while he stirred the stew with a long-handled spoon.

As Li Mei carried a beer tray toward the prospectors' table, the glance of one of the hard cases found her. The man with curly blond hair poking out from beneath a battered brown derby, and sitting at a table near the bar, regarded her wryly, his cold, appraising eyes running up and down the girl's lithe frame. As Li Mei set the beer mugs on the prospectors' table, the blond hard case's eyes sharpened while his near-toothless smile grew, and he poked the brim of his dusty hat off his forehead.

"You gonna deal them cards, or you just gonna stare at the kitchen help?" barked the giant black man sitting to his right.

"Don't get your bloomers in a twist, Brown," the hard case said and, turning his gaze to the other cardplayers, began flipping the pasteboards around the table.

"Hey, Chinaman, you gonna stir that stew all day, or you gonna dish it up?" one of the prospectors said.

Kong jerked his head around. The prospector who'd spoken stared at him expectantly, a fat stogie clamped in his teeth.

Bowing and muttering his apologies, "So sorry, so sorry," Kong quickly scooped stew into four wooden bowls, and delivered the bowls and silverware to the waiting prospectors. He shuffled and bowed, arranged the forks and spoons beside the bowls, then shuffled back to the table by the fireplace to retrieve a loaf of crusty brown bread.

When he'd set the bread on the table, he turned toward the bar, where Gilman was frantically filling mugs from the beer tap and slopping whiskey into shot glasses. Kong stopped suddenly. The lead hard case, standing at the bar, stared angrily toward him, as if trying to see through him.

"Get the hell outta the way, Chinaman." The man with the hummingbird tattoo beneath his milky left eye waved Kong aside. "You're blockin' my view!"

Kong frowned, confused. Shuffling aside, he turned to follow the hard case's stare to one of the prospectors whom Kong had just served. The prospector stared past Kong toward the bar, a steaming spoonful of stew held halfway to his mouth. His eyes grew large, and his bearded faced turned red.

"Lowry Gemmell," said the man with the tattoo, issuing the prospector a rock-hard grin. "Well, well, well."

As the hard case shoved away from the bar and strode toward the prospectors' table, his right hand released the thong over his revolver's hammer.

"Wait a minute now, Cannady," said the prospector, dropping his spoon into his bowl and leaning back in his chair, holding his hands chest high, palms out. "I couldn't come back fer ya. That posse was all over me like ants on honey."

"Boys," yelled the hard case to the rest of the room. "Remember how I told you about an old friend of mine leavin' me out on the Devil's dance floor down Arizony way, with a dead horse, no food, and damn little water?"

"I was gonna bring you back a horse," protested the prospector, sweat runneling his long, blond beard. "Fact, I was headin' back your way with one, but then the damn posse sniffed me out."

"So, that's Lowry Gemmell," said one of the other hard cases, chuckling and shaking his head. "Man, did you cross the wrong hombre!"

Gemmell stared up at Cannady, who stopped before his table. Gemmell's chest rose and fell sharply, and his fingers curled down over his upraised palms. "Now, let's talk this out, Clayton. No reason why two civilized human beings can't iron out a wrinkle in their friendship."

"Yeah, they is," said Cannady. He drew his gun in a single, short blur, and pulled the trigger.

Gemmell rocketed straight back in his chair, hit the floor with a resounding boom.

Cannady grabbed another prospector by his collar, flung him out of his chair, kicked the chair out of his way, and walked over to where Gemmell lay writhing.

" 'Cause one of us is *dead!*"

Cannady's revolver spoke three more times — three angry shots delivered one second apart. The chandeliers rattled and the floor vibrated.

In the ensuing silence, one of the prospectors standing to Gemmell's right, holding a frothy beer mug in his ham-sized right fist, muttered, "Shit."

Kong Zhao had stood frozen beside the square-hewn center post. Now he backed slowly toward his daughter.

5

Kong Zhao was backing toward Li Mei when the gang leader turned his milky left eye on him and jutted his finger. "You, Chinaman, got some trash for you to haul out to the trash heap. Hop-hop. Sing-sing. Pronto!"

The others laughed, breaking the silence following the gunfire.

Cannady turned to the other prospectors sitting at Lowry Gemmell's table. "You boys don't mind, do ya? I mean, this son of a bitch certainly wasn't no friend of *yours,* was he?"

The hard case's voice so teemed with accusation that the other three men stared at him in hang-jawed silence.

"Didn't think so." Cannady turned to Kong. "What'd I tell you, Chinaman? Hop to it! Them trash heap rats and coyotes is hungry!"

Kong glanced at his daughter. He wanted

to tell her to go into the back room or upstairs till these men had left, but he'd only draw attention to her. Maybe, seeing that she was merely Chinese, they'd leave her alone.

Kong nodded and shuffled over to the dead man, whose chest was thickly bibbed with dark red blood and whose eyes seemed to gaze down at something on the floor over his right shoulder. The Chinaman shoved several chairs out of his way and, breathing heavily but moving lightly on his slippered feet, grabbed the dead man under the shoulders and pulled him through the tables toward the building's back door.

When he'd gotten the man outside, a voice from within said, "Tell your China doll to get her ass over here with them beers, barman. My throat's damn dusty and" — the man pinched his voice with mock horror — "my nerves are shot from the sight of all that blood!"

"There, there, Paxton," came another voice. "You're gonna be *just* fine."

Laughter.

Mumbling English curses, Kong Zhao dragged the dead man out past the woodpile toward the creek, and stopped. He straightened, wincing at the pain in his lower back, and sleeved sweat from his forehead.

What to do with the man? He couldn't really throw him in the trash heap. His body would attract dangerous predators, and after a couple of days in the hot sun, the smell would permeate the town.

He looked around. There was no time to bury the man now. Kong couldn't leave his daughter alone in the saloon for that long. He'd leave the man here, and bury him later on the other side of the creek.

That resolved, Kong had begun shuffling back toward the saloon when the sound of galloping hooves from the road on the other side of the building hauled him up short. Angry voices rose. The hooves fell silent. Tack squawked and buckles clanked as men swung down from saddles.

Kong had paused, canting his head to listen. Now he moved forward, opened the saloon's back door, and stepped inside at the same time three big men wearing badges entered the saloon from the front, two armed with double-barreled shotguns.

"What the hell's all the damn shootin' about?" barked the tallest man of the three, holding a rifle over his shoulder. "Heard the shots a half mile out of town." His name was Frank Early. Kong had served the man stew and beer when he'd passed through town before, and seeing the big man and his two deputies, Kong knew a moment's relief.

If anyone could send the hard cases on their way, it was Constable Early and his deputies, Mulroney and Finnigan.

The lead hard case had been turned toward the back of the saloon, talking to the man beside him. Now he swung around without hesitation and said with brash frankness, "I killed a man."

"You did, did you?" said Constable Early, a tall man in a high-crowned black hat and long cream duster. He wore a handlebar mustache with waxed, upturned ends. "My name's Early. I was named constable by this village and the two others up the line. And you are under arrest unless you can convince me you killed in self-defense."

"I didn't kill in no *self-defense*," said Cannady, rising up on the balls of his boots. "I killed Lowry Gemmell because, after him and me done robbed the bank in Prescott six years ago, he left me stranded in the desert east of Yuma. Shot the shirttail lizard straight up, right through his lyin', cheatin' heart. Didn't even give the bastard a chance to draw his weapon."

"So, it's murder then," said one of the other men flanking the constable, raising a double-barreled shotgun high across

65

his chest.

"No, it weren't *murder*," announced the black man sitting at one of the tables, his deep, resonant voice loud enough to be heard at the other end of the settlement. "It was puttin' a low-down dirty dog out of his own mis'ry. Too good for him — too *fast* — if'n you ast me."

The other hard cases whooped and laughed. Several slapped their tables.

In the following silence, the back door clicked open. Kong turned to see another man, wearing a duster and a badge cut from a fruit or vegetable tin, step into the room and cradle a shotgun in his brawny arms. He had a salt-and-pepper mustache turned down over both corners of his mouth, and wore high-topped, brush-gnawed, mule-eared boots. He regarded the room like an angry schoolmaster, eyes slitted and head swiveling slowly from left to right.

"Look out, boys!" cried Cannady at the front of the room. "We're surrounded!"

More laughter.

"I'll see your three," said the black man casually to one of his gambling partners, tossing coins onto the table, "and I'll raise you three more."

Cannady turned to the head lawdog. "As you can see, Mr. Late, you're interruptin' a

66

good time. True, blood has been spilled. But if you don't want any more spilled — namely *your* blood spilled — you best take your little tin stars and light a shuck. Your mommas are callin' you boys. Supper's on the table."

Scowling, Cannady turned slowly back to the table.

"Why, you insolent little snipe!" snarled Early.

From the end of the bar, ready to grab Li Mei standing ten feet to his right with a tray of empty glasses in her hands, Kong saw Cannady snap his head back toward the constable. Kong expected Cannady to say something. To *yell* something. Instead, the Chinaman heard a soft, crunching thud.

Kong blinked and stared over Cannady's right shoulder. A slender knife protruded from the upper middle of Early's chest. The lawman stumbled back toward the saloon's front wall, grunting and hissing and looking down, awestruck, at the blade in his chest.

"Christ!" grunted one of the other lawmen, staring at the injured constable.

As Early dropped to his knees, the other deputy bolted forward, leveling his shotgun at Cannady. "You son of a *bitch!*"

A half second before the deputy pulled the trigger, the black man bolted up from

67

his seat, his fists filled with two stag-butted revolvers. He aimed one, and raked a slug off the deputy's left temple.

Screaming and falling sideways, the deputy triggered one of the two-bore's barrels into the back bar behind Cannady, taking Blacky Gilman through the dead middle of his white-shirted chest. The blast threw the barman back against the shelves, knocking bottles and glasses to and fro and down with a screaming clatter of broken glass.

Kong heard pounding boot falls behind him. He half turned to see the man who'd entered via the back door run up through the middle of the room, screaming, "Stand down, you sons o' bitches, or —"

Several pistol shots cut him off, the slugs tearing through both shoulders. He stumbled over a chair and fell forward.

Ka-boom!

His scattergun sounded like a cannon.

Several men near the front of the room shouted curses and scrambled for cover as the pellets shredded the air like enraged bumblebees. Several bits of shot shattered a lit bracket lamp on the center post, and fire rained down with the kerosene like the breath of a low-flying dragon.

Whoosh!

Pistols popped. Men screamed and

whooped. The deputy at the front of the room, blood trickling down from his grooved temple, gained his feet and bull-charged the black man, stretching the shotgun straight out from his belly.

The shotgun's blast rocked the room, but Kong didn't look to see if the man had hit his mark. The room was fast filling with smoke and flames, and the Chinaman found himself in a headlong dive toward his daughter. Li Mei had dropped her tray of glasses, and crouched down behind an overturned chair, clamping her hands to her ears. Kong hooked his left arm around her shoulders, and threw her to the floor as several stray pistol shots smashed the chair she'd been crouched behind.

Covering his daughter's body with his own, Kong reached up and pulled a table down before them, shielding them from the spanging, ricocheting bullets. He lowered his cheek to Li Mei's and held it there, feeling the girl sob and shake beneath him, while the whoops and pistol shots continued for what seemed an eternity.

As the smoke grew thicker, Li Mei began to convulse and cough. Kong ripped the bandanna from around his neck, and held it over the girl's mouth and nose. When the gunfire died, he lifted a glance over the table. The flames leapt across the floor to lick at the rafters. Vague human shapes flickered through the smoke.

Above the fire's roar, a man shouted, "You have enough now, Mr. Constable, sir? No? Well, here then." Two more shots ripped above the fire's hum and crackle. "Have a couple more!"

Boots thumped.

A man cursed in a pinched, pained voice.

"Come on, boys, let's get the hell outta here!"

Kong looked to his left and behind. The fire had streaked along the bar toward the back door, but he and Li Mei could make it if they went now.

"Come, daughter," he yelled in English, the language that, to the Chinaman's chagrin, his daughter understood the best. "We must go." He rose and pulled the girl to her feet. "Keep the cloth over your mouth!"

He turned toward the door and began pulling Li Mei along behind. Suddenly, the girl's arm slipped out of his hand.

"Li Mei!" the Chinaman cried, turning.

A man stood before him, crouched over Li Mei, who'd dropped to one knee. "Oh, no, you don't, ye greasy cockroach! This girl's comin' with me!"

As the man jerked Li Mei brusquely to

70

her feet, the girl screamed and fought. The man, whose curly blond hair poked out from beneath his shabby bowler, held fast to Li Mei's arm and raised a cocked pistol toward Kong.

"No!"

The girl's scream was drowned out by the pistol's roar. Fire burned in the Chinaman's temple as he staggered backward and fell, his back hitting the floor with a thunderous boom.

He lay staring at the smoky ceiling, his limbs going heavy and numb, cannons booming in his head. He gritted his teeth.

Li Mei.

He lifted his head from the floor, blinked several times. Into the broiling smoke, the blond hard case retreated, heading for the front of the fire-filled room, dragging Li Mei along behind him.

6

Cuno Massey hauled the four dead hard cases away from Columbine in the back of a buckboard wagon that he borrowed from the livery barn. When he figured he was far enough away from the town that the stench wouldn't pester the girls at Miss Mundy's, he dumped the four carcasses without ceremony into a deep ravine.

Only the cooling evening breeze said a few words. The only thing covering the makeshift grave was the fast-approaching shadows bleeding out from the western rimrocks.

Flies buzzed. Magpies lighted on rocks above the carrion, scrutinizing the corpses, their tiny, black eyes bulging with expectation.

Cuno took a long pull from his canteen. He returned the cork to the spout and peered once more into the ravine. The naked hard case with the long, blond locks lay twisted atop two of the three other dead men, skinny legs scissored, arms stretched straight out from his shoulders. The man's bloody mouth still shaped a surprised O. The third body had snugged up to a boulder as though to a comely whore; one of the magpies had already lighted on his shoulder.

"Don't worry," Cuno told the skinny gent with the long blond hair, sleeving sweat from his brow. "Your brother will be along soon."

Cuno spat into the cleft, snugged his hat down tight, and headed back to the wagon.

When he'd returned the buckboard to the livery barn, he dragged Wade Scanlon's coffin to a quiet place behind Parker's barn, and began digging a grave by the light of a bull's-eye lantern. While he dug, Parker came out and played his fiddle — quiet, mournful tunes blending with the strains of the night breeze sliding over the Rockies.

Cuno and the old man lowered the coffin and filled in the hole. The last rays of the sun had retreated, and full night had closed down — cool, dark, and star-sprinkled.

Parker recited the Lord's Prayer, holding his fiddle under his arm, his bow hanging straight down at his side, chin tipped to his chest. When the old man was finished, Cuno donned his hat and stared at the mounded grave. His jaw tightened.

He and Wade Scanlon had met in a Denver saloon after Cuno had moved out West from Nebraska. Because he had only one leg, Scanlon couldn't find work besides sweeping out saloons and mucking out livery barns. Flush with poker winnings, he partnered up with Cuno, and in ten months, they'd become best friends.

Now, Cuno set Scanlon's weather-battered hat down on his grave. He picked up Scanlon's crutch and broke it over his knee. Tossing it into the brush, he said, "You won't be needing that anymore, Wade. Wherever you are, I know you got both legs again."

He put in place the cross he'd fashioned from two pine branches and rawhide, then grabbed the shovel and started back toward the saloon.

Serenity Parker's voice rose behind him. "Miss Lara's waitin' fer ya, over to Miss Mundy's. There's a bottle on the bar. It's for you and her."

"Thanks," Cuno said, walking away. "Not tonight."

He grabbed his camping gear from the barn, where his wagon was parked, his mules milling in the side corral, then walked out to the creek and built a small fire in an aspen grove. He stripped down, waded into the creek, and bathed the sweat and grime from his broad-shouldered, slim-hipped body.

He found a deep pool between two boulders, and sat down to let the chill water rush over him, then waded back to shore. He lay down naked on his bedroll, letting the cool air dry him. Propped on one shoulder, he filled a tin cup with coffee and rolled a smoke.

Resting his head against a tree, bare ankles crossed, he smoked and stared at the stars beyond the nodding limbs of an aspen.

Death had hit him so many times — his parents, his stepmother, his beautiful young wife, July, and their unborn child. Puzzling how it affected him now. Not so much sorrow as a hollowed-out feeling. Emptiness. Like an old corncob still swaying on a reed-like stock, all the kernels long since eaten by crows.

He was only twenty-three years old. . . .

He took a deep drag from the quirley, tipped his head back to blow smoke at the stars.

Wade gone now too. His only friend. The loss of Wade's freight meant Cuno wouldn't take in enough profit to buy more goods for another haul. He'd have to sell his wagon and his other two mules just to stake himself through the winter.

It was either that or hire out his gun. An unappealing prospect, but maybe that's what was waiting for him. God knows he'd killed enough men with the .45 he'd been given by the old pistoleer, Charlie Dodge, who himself had been crippled during a lead swap.

Charlie had taught Cuno how to shoot when Cuno had begun fogging the trail of his father and stepmother's killers, Anderson and Spoon. Charlie had done a good job. Cuno had killed both men, and the others who'd then come after Cuno, including bounty killers and would-be pistoleers seeking reputations of their own.

No, he couldn't go back to that. It didn't matter how good he'd become at it, how used to it. Killing to avoid death was no way to live. Once he'd settled this current score, and avenged Wade, he'd hang up his guns for good.

He tapped ashes from the quirley. Shit, he'd probably be mucking out barn stalls come December, the very work old Wade himself had been running from.

A twig snapped. Cuno dropped the coffee cup and grabbed his .45 snugged in the holster coiled to his right. A second after the cup had dropped with a ping, the smell of scorched java rising, he flicked the Colt's hammer back and aimed the gun in the direction from which the sound had come.

"It's me."

Cuno released the hammer, canted the Colt's barrel up, and draped a corner of his bedroll across his naked crotch. Not that Lara hadn't seen him naked before. He'd shared her bed over at Miss Mundy's his first time through Columbine, and all four times since. No particular reason why he slept with whores; he could have had his pick of single, respectable women in Denver. Maybe lying with whores didn't seem quite so much like cheating on July.

Now, holding a wrapper closed at her throat with one hand, the girl stepped out of the shadows — a lithe figure with a pale, heart-shaped face, blond hair piled loosely atop her head. "What're you bein' so stand-offish about tonight?"

"When I'm feelin' this ornery, I ain't fit company." He set the gun aside. "No offense."

"You shouldn't be alone. You just lost a friend."

She lifted the wrapper's hem above her bare knees and sat down beside him, curling her slender legs beneath her hip and leaning on her hand. The wrapper spread

77

open, revealing nearly all of one pale breast, a tiny mole showing at the top of her cleavage.

"All the more reason," he said.

She glanced at the creek, then turned her face back toward his. Her voice was quiet, shy. "I don't mind telling you, Cuno, I sure have treasured your trips through Columbine. I've taken a shine to you, in fact. If you want me to go, I'll go. But if you want me to stay, I wouldn't take any money for it tonight." She held his gaze. "Or any night, comes to that."

He rose to a kneeling position, wrapping the blanket around his waist, knotting it behind his back, and poured a cup of coffee for them both. He handed one to the girl, who took it, staring up at him.

"I reckon this'll be my last time through."

She dropped her eyes as she held the cup in both hands in her lap. "Well, I'm sorry to hear that."

Cuno sat down against the tree and crossed his ankles. "You know, Miss Lara, if there was a girl I'd be ready to settle down with again, she'd be you."

Her eyes flickered hopefully in the firelight. "You'd settle down with a whore?"

He leaned toward her, resting on his elbow, letting the blanket fall away from his waist. He placed his hands gently against her face, caressed her cheek with his fingers, relishing the soft, supple skin. "I'd settle down with you."

He meant it.

"The time ain't right, I reckon."

He shook his head.

"Because you're going after the men who killed Wade?"

"That," Cuno said, "and because I don't know what lies ahead after that. If there is an afterward."

"How does anybody know what lies ahead?"

"It's not just that."

She glanced at the .45 snugged in his holster. "You gonna take it up again? Shootin'?"

"How'd you know I ever did?"

"No one could have taken those four gunnies down the way you did less'n they was practiced at it."

Cuno pulled his hand away from her face. "I'm sorry."

"You don't have nothin' to be sorry about. No more than I do. I just wish we could be together, that's all. I been at this trade for two years, since my parents were killed in a stage holdup, and no man has ever treated me half as gentle as you." She leaned toward him, kissed him gently; her lips were soft and sweet. "Made me feel as good as you."

He took her in his arms, lifted her onto his lap, kissing her and running his hands up and down her back, pressing her close. She wrapped her legs around his waist. He pushed her gently back, unbuttoned the wrapper, and slid it down her arms, both erect nipples popping free, the pale, pear-shaped breasts glowing umber in the fire-light.

He leaned down, kissed each breast, then kissed her lips again while gently turning onto his left side, sliding her beneath him. She opened her legs for him and, entering her, he leaned on his outstretched arms, his big, red-brown hands splayed out on either side of her head. The cords and heavy muscles in his arms stretched taut.

She raised her knees to his sides. Her fingers caressed his shoulders, raising goose-flesh, as he plunged down deep inside her.

"Ohhhh," she cooed. "Ah! Gawd!"

Cuno woke the next morning before first light, the dawn a purple glow in the east. Lara lay curled beside him, her face buried in his armpit, one bare leg curled over his right thigh. Her soft, moist breath tickled slightly, stirred his loins for a moment.

No time for that.

He swung the blankets off him, slid quietly away from her, stood, covered her pale, curled body with the blanket, and dressed. He washed his face in the river, a bracing wash of cold mountain water, numbing his vague, nagging desire. He turned back to her still curled beneath his heavy, striped Indian blankets that they'd needed when it had turned cold last night.

He had to get moving, get an early start. He was far enough behind Wade's killers as it was. If his freight hadn't been due in Welcome by Saturday, he'd have rented a fast horse, completed his grisly business, and ridden back for the wagon later.

He walked back to Lara, crouched down, and lifted her into his arms. She moaned, and her eyelids fluttered. She wrapped her arms around his neck, pressed her cheek against his shoulder, and went back to sleep.

Cuno carried her around the fire and through the trees toward the yard, the damp grass and sage crackling softly beneath his tread. As he walked past the livery barn, he stopped and turned to Serenity Parker standing outside his saloon, the sashed window dimly lit on either side of him. Smoke wafted from the saloon's tin chimney pipe, smelling like eggs, pork, and coffee.

"Breakfast?" Parker said quietly.

Cuno shook his head. "No time."

"Beware of Long Draw," Parker warned. "Bad place these days. Road agents and such."

Cuno nodded and continued to the brothel's overgrown yard, mounted the steps, and pushed inside. The cloying smell of whiskey and tobacco smoke followed him through the dark, quiet parlor, where one girl slept on a fainting couch, and up the stairs, the carpeted planks creaking beneath his boots. From somewhere came a man's low voice and a girl's quiet laughter. One of the customers already up, charming one of the girls.

The hall was dark, but Cuno saw Lara's bedroom door standing ajar on the other side of the cuckoo clock. Inside the small room, he crouched with the girl in his arms, pulled the sheet and blankets back, and gentled her onto the bed.

She sighed and pressed her cheek to the pillow, rolling onto her side, facing Cuno, and bringing her knees toward her chest. As he raised the blankets, he saw her toes flex and curl.

"Are you going?" she whispered.

"Uh-huh."

"Don't go. Stay here with me."

He kissed her cheek, pressed his forehead to hers. He stayed there for a moment, taking a deep breath, smelling the warm, peach smell of the girl. He'd like to remember it for later, when things got ugly again. You needed something like the smell of a woman, or the image of a sun-dappled creek with mayflies hatching, to maintain sanity when the shit started flying.

So that you remembered there were other things in life besides death and killing.

He kissed her once more, squeezed her shoulder, and moved to the door. He stopped, plucked a piece of silver from his front pocket, began to set it on the dresser, and stopped. He turned back to Lara breathing softly under the blankets, the window behind her turning pale.

He returned the silver to his pocket, went out, and quietly closed the door.

7

Cuno let himself out of Miss Mundy's and headed for the livery barn. It was still dark, but the horses and mules were scuffling around the corral, knowing it was getting close to chow time. Cuno walked around behind the barn, retrieved his camping gear from the creek, then walked back to the barn. He was opening the small front door when he turned toward Serenity Parker's saloon and paused.

The windows were dark. A CLOSED sign hung in the right front window. The old man must've decided to take the day off and go fishing.

Cuno continued into the barn, tossed his gear into the wagon box, behind the driver's seat, then went out to fetch his mules. A half hour later, he was moving along the gently sloping wagon road west of Columbine, watching his shadow angling out ahead of him along the rocky ground, the copper sun rising from the sage of the eastern flats behind him. On his left, Columbine Creek gurgled in its steep cut, sheathed in willows and aspens, pines and cedars studding the canyon's boulder-strewn walls rising to either side of the lumbering wagon.

Around ten, the sun heated up, reflecting off the canyon walls, and Cuno slipped out of his denim jacket, tossed it into the box behind him. He was about to reach into his grub sack for some biscuits when a shadow flicked in the corner of his right eye, up high on a towering scarp. A rifle barked, the shot plunking into the seat a foot from Cuno's right thigh.

The mule spooked to the right of the trail, and the wagon's right front wheel slammed between two low boulders, giving a wooden crunch. The mule brayed as another rifle shot spanged off one of the boulders. The animal put its head down to lunge ahead, but the wagon held fast.

Cuno grabbed his rifle, jacked a round into the chamber, aimed at the scarp's crest, and fired. The man there ducked down behind a cedar as Cuno's .44 slug kicked up dirt just below the tree.

As several more rifles barked around him, kicking up dirt and gravel and chewing pieces from the wagon, Cuno leapt left off the wagon. He landed on a flat-topped boulder a few feet down the creek's ravine, turned a quick glance back toward the road. Three men were hunkered down behind rocks ahead of the wagon, crouching behind boulders and cedars a third of the way up the canyon wall.

Cuno fired three quick shots, saw a bush-whacker grab his shoulder and fall behind his cover, dropping his rifle. As the road agents returned fire, Cuno leapt from the boulder into the aspens and ran and slid down the slope toward the creek, loosing clay and gravel in his wake.

Damn fool, he chided himself. So busy thinking about Wade's killers, wondering how to make up the road time, that he hadn't realized he'd entered Long Draw, which all eastern slope freighters knew had recently become a favorite haunt of road agents.

At the edge of the water, Cuno hunkered down behind a cottonwood. He doffed his hat, threw it down to his feet. Keeping his head and cocked rifle back behind the tree trunk, he waited, listening.

Footsteps sounded. A rustling of brush, the clatter of rock. Pressing his back to the rough cottonwood bark, he glanced to his right. A shadow moved along the bank, scuttling across the adobe-colored stones.

Moving quickly, he snaked the rifle around the right side of the trunk and fired. The man, who'd come halfway down the bank, gave a surprised grunt, staggering back. Regaining his balance, he raised his revolver and fired, the shot plunking into the cottonwood. Cuno flinched, rammed a fresh shell into the Winchester's chamber, and returned fire, the .44 round blowing up sand between the bushwhacker's boots.

Cuno bolted out from behind the tree as the man scurried back up the bank, moving sideways and up toward the road and a small cottonwood copse. Gritting his teeth, Cuno took aim, fired two more quick shots, blowing up dust at the buchwhacker's feet. The third shot sliced between the man's scissoring legs as he gained the crest, smacking the inside of his left thigh.

The man groaned and hopped sideways, dropping his pistol and clutching his left leg. He dropped onto the road and out of Cuno's line of vision.

"Simms!" a man shouted.

Thrashing rose from the road, the scuff of boot heels. A pinched voice: "He's down by the river!"

Cuno saw two more heads and rifle barrels moving along the road, on the other side of the trees. Dusters flapped back like devils' wings. Cuno scrambled out from behind the cottonwood, moving left, upstream, toward a deep cleft in the bank. Over the cleft was a slight ledge, where falling rock had hung up against old tree roots.

He scrambled into the cut, which was high enough that he could stand and only bow his head slightly. He was hidden from anyone descending the bank either upstream or down. Slowly, stretching his lips in a wince, he levered another shell into the firing chamber. He leaned the rifle barrel up against the bank beside him, unholstered his Colt .45, and checked to make sure all chambers showed brass.

He holstered the .45, picked up his rifle, and waited.

Voices rolled down from the road. A few minutes later, stones rolled down the bank to Cuno's right. A few plopped into the water, the splashes drowned by the stream's tinny rush.

A shadow flashed on the gold-dappled stream. Cuno pressed his back as far into the cleft as he could, looking to both sides, making sure he cast no shadow on the bank.

Minutes passed. He was about to risk a peek along the bank, when sand dribbled off the ledge just above his head. It sifted down near the squared toes of his low-heeled boots.

He lifted his eyes to the ledge, the hair on the back of his neck prickling. A cunning light entered his eyes, and he almost sneered. He took a breath, squeezed the rifle in his hands, then took one step away from the cleft, moving toward the river before swinging around toward the bank, raising his rifle.

Another bushwhacker stood atop the cleft, one boot resting on a thickly knotted root jutting from the ledge — a tall, latigo-tough hombre with pale hair falling down from his coffee-colored Stetson, a Winchester carbine in his beringed hands.

He saw Cuno too late. His eyes snapped wide, and he began moving his carbine down. Cuno's Winchester barked. The man dropped his rifle to grab his lower chest with both hands, his cheeks bulging, eyes pinching.

Cuno reached up with his left hand, gave the man's right leg a tug. The man tumbled off the ledge and hit the ground in a cloud of puffing dust and falling stones. Cuno picked him up by his collar, feeling the man's death spasms through his wrist, and threw him into the stream.

The body skidded off a couple of water-polished rocks, then turned onto its back, the boots still kicking, the water roiling red. The body turned this way and that before the current caught it and hauled it, bobbing and rocking, hands flung out, palms up, downstream.

Rip Webber was hunkered in the cottonwoods near the wagon, his rifle resting across his thighs, when he saw something floating down creek. He squinted his eyes. A deer maybe — a small doe or fawn that had fallen and drowned when trying to cross the stream.

Then he saw the man's body — Liddy Lewis — twisting and turning, the water red-tinged around it before it swept over a small beaver dam and shot headfirst downstream. It turned a semicircle before disappearing around a bend.

"Christ," Webber said, running his eyes upriver. Seeing no more signs of the driver, he rose and walked up the road.

Donny Simms was still writhing around in the middle of the trail, trying to knot a neckerchief around his thigh. Joe Zorn was making his way down the ridge on the other side of the trail, cupping a bloody hand to his shoulder, holding his rifle low along his fringed right chap. His hatchet face was set grimly beneath the broad brim of his hat.

Stopping near Simms, Webber looked up the road. Fletcher Updike was hunkered behind a boulder, peering into the river cut, squeezing his Spencer rifle as though trying to ring water from a soaked towel.

"You see him?" Webber called.

Updike turned his round face toward him, shook his head.

Webber glanced at the river, ran a hand across his jaw, feeling foolish at having been hornswoggled by a mere freighter — the freighter he and his four partners had themselves intended to hornswoggle — then turned again to Updike.

"Let's get the wagon and light a shuck."

"What about that son of a bitch down there?" Updike called. "I think he killed Liddy."

"He did kill Liddy, you tinhorn." Webber's thick nostrils swelled. "We go after him, he'll kill us too. I know when I'm beat, and when to light a shuck, and I been beat here, so I'm lightin' a shuck."

Joe Zorn leapt from a rock to the road, grunting painfully. "At least we got the wagon. Who was that son of a bitch anyway?"

"Some freighter that don't like givin' up his load," Webber said as, walking toward the wagon, he ran his gloved hand over one of the mule's backs, appraising the beast. He could get a hundred and fifty for the mule over at Lyons. "Help me get the wagon unstuck, and let's get the hell out of here."

Trying to push himself up on his good leg, Donny Simms shouted, "Give me a hand, goddamnit!"

Ignoring him, Webber walked to the rear of the wagon. He cast his glance over the covered load, and removed one of the ropes tied over the tarp. "Gonna have me a look inside, see what that short-trigger freighter done donated." He chuckled, cast another nervous glance into the creek gorge, then removed another rope.

When Zorn had removed the ropes hooked to steel eyes on the far side of the wagon box, the men each took a side of the tarp, lifted it, and peered over the tailgate.

KAA-BOOM!

Joe Zorn's head instantly vaporized, blood spraying behind the wagon like red paint.

"No!" shouted Webber.

KAA-BOOM!

The blast took him through the chest, lifting him straight up in the air and six feet straight back. He hit the ground, arms and legs spasming, his eyes already glassy.

Cuno was halfway up the riverbank, moving toward the wagon, when he'd heard the shotgun blasts and the man's shout. Cuno stopped, listening and wondering as the twin echoes chased each other around the canyon. He heard running footfalls, then scrambled up the bank, pulling at weed clumps and fixed rocks, no longer caring how much noise he made.

He'd just lifted his head above the road's crest when a man ran past him from left to right, heading for the wagon fifty feet away.

Cuno crouched and leveled his Winchester. "Hold it!"

The man skidded, stopped, and swung around with his Spencer. Cuno drilled him twice through the chest, then flinched as a bullet sliced across his own left temple.

He whirled, saw a slumped figure in the road, and triggered the Winchester twice more. One round smacked through the man's left hand resting on the ground before ricocheting off the rock beneath it. The second plunked through his right cheekbone and smashed him straight back on the trail, flopping like a landed fish.

Cuno ejected the smoking shell casing, levered another into the chamber, and swung the Winchester's barrel around, looking for more shooters. The mules were braying and bobbing their heads, trying to plunge forward through the rocks, but to no avail. The wheels held fast. The animals and a single, high-hunting hawk made the only sounds, the only movements.

"Oh, Christ!" A man's voice rose from the wagon. There was a dull thump and a wooden clatter, as of something hitting the ground. "Mercy!"

Staying to the opposite side of the trail, Cuno ran down the side of the wagon, stopped, and aimed the Winchester toward the back. The tailgate was open. Lying twisted and groaning on the ground beneath it, clutching his left knee with both hands, was Serenity Parker. His shotgun, both barrels smoking, lay over the leg of one of the two dead men.

"Christalmighty, Parker, what in the hell are you doing here?"

"Flyin' whores!" Parker gritted his teeth. "Hurt my knee."

"Can you stand?"

"Give me a second." He clutched the knee for a time, slowly released it. Even more slowly, he stretched the leg out, then glanced at Cuno. "Give me a hand."

Cuno took the Winchester in his left hand, offered his right to the old man, gingerly helped the man to his feet. Parker stood,

94

testing his weight on his right knee, then gently flexed it.

"Think it'll be all right now."

"What the hell were you doing in my wagon?"

The old man looked sheepish, but as he glanced around at the two men he'd nearly obliterated with his gut shredder, he gained a look of surprise and admiration. "I reckon you could call me a stowaway."

"If you wanted a ride somewhere, you could have asked me for one. You didn't need to hide under the tarp."

The old man walked around, limping, testing the knee. He walked over to Webber, stooped with a grunt, trying to bend only his left knee, and picked up the shotgun. He wiped the blood-flecked stock on his thigh.

"I reckon I ain't really goin' anywhere. I mean, I'm goin' where you're goin'." He broke open the shotgun, plucked out the spent wads, and fished two more out of the breast pocket of his worn flannel shirt, nudging aside a suspender strap.

Cuno squinted one eye and grunted, "You're going where I'm going."

"I'm goin' after those killers, same as you," the old man said, shoving the fresh wads into both shotgun barrels. "I didn't do right by ole Wade. I froze up. Damnit, I peed my pants!" He stopped, pursed his lips. A tear rolled down from his right eye. "I just stood there inside my saloon and watched through the doors while they looted his wagon and shot him like a damn dog on the boardwalk."

He looked up at Cuno, both eyes shiny now, his gaunt, bearded face crimson with rage. "I'm goin' after 'em, same as you, and I'm gonna give 'em my two cents' worth." He closed the gun with a metallic snap. "For Wade."

Cuno held his gaze. "How far were you going to ride in the back?"

"Till we were far enough from Columbine you wouldn't send me back afoot."

Cuno turned, set his rifle on the open tailgate, and walked around the right side of the wagon, scrutinizing the wheels that stood nearly as tall as he. The back one looked all right, but the right front would need its rim reshaped when he found a blacksmith. The felloe might be cracked, but he'd worry about that when it gave out. He hoped it didn't give out on the down side of a steep hill, but he could have thrown a wheel and busted an axle pin and lost a day making repairs.

The old man stood beside the trail, cradling his shotgun in his arms with a defiant expression. Cuno dragged Webber and Zorn across the trail, and kicked them both into the ravine, their bodies rolling down and splashing water at the edge of the stream. When he'd disposed of the other two bodies, he settled the mules down with handfuls of cracked corn, then backed them slowly out of the rocks and onto the trail.

The back wheel turned smoothly. The front one gave a slight thump as the bent rim hit the ground, but the felloe held.

Cuno checked the straps and buckles, then grabbed his shotgun and climbed into the driver's box. He released the brake and looked over his left shoulder. The old man stood regarding him from the shade of the cottonwoods, his defiant expression tempered with wariness.

"Well?" Cuno said.

The old man pursed his lips, adjusted his suspenders with a shrug of his shoulders, then walked around behind the wagon and slid his shotgun onto the floor of the driver's box. He gingerly climbed the wheel, and sat in the seat beside Cuno.

He stared straight ahead. "How come you ain't balkin'?"

" 'Cause it's too damn far from Columbine to turn out an old fool." Cuno clucked to the mules, shook the reins.

The mules leaned into their collars. The wagon rolled forward.

8

Late that same day, when the sun had fallen over the Front Range and cold shadows bled down from the high peaks, "The Committee" rode into the little river-crossing settlement of Danger Ford.

Danger Ford Creek was far from dangerous this time of the year, long after the spring rains that often made it so. And the piano clattering in the sprawling whorehouse called Heaven's Bane, atop a bluff on the creek's south side, cast a downright gay ambience over the steep-walled canyon.

The chill air, bespeaking fall, was perfumed with pine smoke from the whorehouse, the miners' shacks and tents sheathing the creek, and the mountain diggings up and down the gorge. There was also the usual mining-camp fetor of trash heaps, privies, and butchered deer and elk carcasses.

As The Committee crossed the broad

plank bridge over the rushing creek, the horses' shod hooves clattering like cannon blasts, two young boys, fishing along the creek, jerked their worms from the water and, casting frightened looks over their shoulders, ran toward a stone hut crouched in hemlocks and cedars.

Whooping and howling like wolves, the gang climbed the shelves rising to the bluff upon which the whorehouse sat, its windows glowing yellow against the purple twilight. Riding at the head of the group, Waco and El Lobo triggered pistols into the air. The big black man, Ed Brown, guffawed at some joke the man riding beside him, Ned Crockett, had told.

When Clayton Cannady had pulled his horse up to the hitch racks before the broad front porch set atop high, wide steps, he turned to regard the group gathering in the yard behind him. He ordered Waco and El Lobo to holster their pistols, to quit acting like tinhorns, and to stable the gangs' mounts in the barn.

As he began to dismount, he cast a glance back the way he and the others had come, and froze, staring. Sunflower Paxton rode slowly up the last rise, the young Chink girl riding wedged between the blond hard case and his saddle horn. The girl's head sagged between her shoulders. She was half-asleep, terrified and exhausted from travel.

Cannady's voice was sharp. "Paxton, I thought I told you to give that girl the send-off and toss her in a ravine. She's slowin' you down."

As the lathered, hang-headed horse approached the group, Paxton shrugged. "What's the hurry, Boss?"

"That roan is tired. Look at him. He ain't big enough to carry double, even a girl small as her. Now, grow some sense, will you, or I'm gonna give *you* the send-off just for actin' stupid."

"Ah, come on, Cannady. I ain't had her yet, and you know I'm partial to slanty-eyes. Besides, after I've had my fill of her, I'll sell her to one of these lonely prospectors, make some extry cash."

The Indian, Young Knife, walked over to Paxton's horse, reached up to brush the girl's hair back from her face, and roughly grabbed the back of her neck to stare into her eyes. As Li Mei howled and tried to pull away, the Indian grinned, his black gums showing.

"Shit, you might sell her to me, Sunflower. I *like* skinny women with slits for eyes." He rubbed his belly and laughed. "Most Injun women very fat!"

"With big asses too!" said Ned Crockett, chuckling and tossing his horse's reins to Waco, who had gathered a good half dozen already.

"There, you see, Boss?" Paxton said to Cannady. He slipped down from his saddle and turned to the gang leader still sitting his own stallion. "This girl's in high demand around here."

"Why bother with her?" said the old graybeard called Whinnie. Having dismounted and turned his horse over to El Lobo, he was brushing dust from his brush-scarred chaps, his necklace of dried human ears — the ears of a posse that had once trailed him — flopping around his hairy, naked chest. He wore only a thin deer-hide vest, with no shirt underneath, and two big, stag-gripped pistols jutted high on both hips. "Shit, once we get our hands on that mine money in Sundance, you won't —"

The graybeard clipped his sentence when Li Mei kicked her left slippered foot into Paxton's throat, shrieking like an Asian witch. As Paxton staggered back, she reached down, grabbed the reins, slid back in the saddle, jabbed her heels into the roan's ribs, and screamed, "Gooo!"

The tired horse leapt off its rear hooves and bounded forward. As it lit out across the yard between the whorehouse and the barn, its right shoulder slammed into Whinnie. The graybeard flew sideways, bellowing and clawing at one of his .44s.

The others scrambled out of the way, yelling and cursing.

"Christalmighty, shoot that bitch!" ordered Cannady, holding his stallion's reins in one hand and thumbing his Smith & Wesson's hammer back.

Paxton knelt on the ground, trying to suck wind down his battered throat, so he didn't see the girl gallop to the other end of the yard, kicking the horse's ribs and screaming, her long, black hair whipping in the wind. When she saw only a corral, several wagons, and a high, shelving hill in her path, she turned the horse and raced back the way she'd come. She tried to skirt the milling gang members, several of whom were laughing by now, several more expounding angrily and aiming revolvers.

"Don't shoot!" railed the big Negro, Ed Brown, as he bounded sideways, slamming his right fist into the palm of his left hand and throwing a shoulder against the racing roan's left stirrup. "Might hit the horse!"

The horse and the girl screamed in unison. The horse stumbled sideways and, throwing the girl out over its left shoulder, fell hard and rolled. The stirrups flapped like the wings of a crazy bat. Dust, gravel, saddlebags, and bedroll flew.

The stallion lay on its side for a moment, blowing, its ribs expanding and contracting, as though in shock. Finally, the horse gained its feet with a groan, shook itself, the saddle falling beneath its belly, and trotted away.

Behind it, near the barn, the girl lay in a pile.

She was breathing sharply, groaning and trying to push herself up with her hands, but her head remained on the ground, her skirts bunch up around her butt, exposing her white bloomers, thin brown legs, white socks, and slippers.

Hushed silence.

Several of the men chuckled softly, like schoolboys after a prank.

"She dead?" growled Whinnie, shaking his frizzy, gray hair back from his hoop earrings as he moved toward her, both long-barreled Starr revolvers drawn. "I hope she ain't, 'cause she's got my name tattooed on her skinny ass now."

Sunflower Paxton beat the old man over to Li Mei, and stood staring down at her. His chest rose and fell sharply, his fists balled at his thighs.

"Say what you want," Ned Crockett said

from the whorehouse's front porch, onto which several men from inside had gathered to see what all the commotion was about. "The girl can ride!"

Snickers.

Paxton heard Whinnie click one of his hammers back. The blond firebrand wheeled, filling his hand so quickly with his own revolver that Whinnie stopped dead in his tracks, hang-jawed.

"Get the fuck back!" Paxton raged, crouched and swinging his Colt around the crowd of onlookers. "Get the fuck *back!*"

Whinnie stood frozen, gaping. Finally, he depressed his Starr's hammer, lowered both revolvers, and stepped back. "Easy, boy."

Paxton was breathing so sharply through his nose, his lips pinched tight, that you could have heard him on the other side of the creek. "She's *mine!*"

The crowd fell silent. Inside, the piano was no longer playing. Silhouetted faces appeared in the windows.

"Boys, stand down," Cannady ordered mildly.

Paxton took a deep breath, holstered his Colt, then reached down and jerked the girl to her feet. She sobbed and groaned, her hair hanging in her face, as Paxton half-dragged, half-carried her through the parting crowd and up the whorehouse's broad front steps. Several men scrambled out of the doorway to let him pass.

Paxton pulled the girl inside and left the door hanging wide behind him.

"Well," drawled Crockett, smoking a stogie on the front porch, "I reckon that girl's about to learn a lesson."

When Paxton and the Chink had disappeared upstairs and the horses were led away to the livery barn, the other men filed into the whorehouse, politely scraping their boots on the hemp mat before the front door, and doffing their hats.

Cannady turned to Crockett, who was smoking beside an awning post. "I don't know about you, Ned, but I could use an ash-haulin'."

"You come to the right place fer it. I heard the Heaven's Bane is *the* place in these parts."

As Crockett carefully mashed out the cigar against the post, saving it for later, Cannady headed for the front door, from which the clatter of piano music was again issuing — a jovial, Old World waltz. Girls laughed, and glasses clinked. Cannady was about to step over the threshold when a hand reached toward him, shoving him brusquely back.

A gruff voice spoke. "We don't cotton to smelly Texicans around these parts . . . stinkin' the place up."

Cannady turned his head right. A man a couple of inches taller than Cannady stood beside the front door, nearly concealed by the shadows between the door and a tall window framed inside by pink curtains. The man was straight-backed and heavy-shouldered and wearing a high-crowned felt sombrero. A sandy mustache drooped over his broad mouth.

He must have seen Cannady's jaws lock, felt the heat rise in Cannady's cheeks. He chuckled affably, lightly punched the outlaw leader's left shoulder. "Ah, smooth your neck hairs down, ye proddy ole bush-whacker. It's Karl Burdette."

Cannady stared at the man, chuffed, and relaxed his fists.

Burdette laughed softly, his yokelike shoulders shuddering behind his red-and-white checked shirt. His black neckerchief, pierced by a turquoise-studded pin and too small for his neck, appeared about to choke him.

Cannady stepped back, glanced at Crockett standing behind him, wary-eyed. "Ned, this is Karl 'The Crocodile' Burdette."

"No shit?"

"Willie and Alfred's brother. They done set up this whole bank thing in Sundance."

"Burdette," muttered Crockett thoughtfully, studying the broad-shouldered gent. "You weren't the one that shot my cousin, Lloyd Petersen, is you? During that riverboat shindig in St. Pete?"

"Hell, no," said Burdette, his sandy brows closing down over his deep, dark eyes. "That was my cousin, Ramsey. I done killed Ramsey near five years ago now, 'cause he sold me out to the federal law in Galveston and I done two years. I apologize if he wronged ye just the same, on account o' he was family."

"Where's the others?" Cannady asked.

"Willie and Alfred's in Sundance, playin' like they're sheriff's deputies." Burdette got a chuckle out of that. "I'm here with Case Oddfellow. You remember him from that Brazos job? We was supposed to meet you and your boys here, give you the lowdown. Case is upstairs gettin' a French lesson. I already had me one and, jumpin' Jehovah, do I recommend 'em!"

"Do believe I'll find me a gal, if they ain't all taken up by now," said Crockett. "You boys can give me the lay o' the land later, eh?"

"Sure thing, partner, but don't go con-

108

tractin' no goat burn!" Cannady cautioned, clapping Crockett on the back. "I'd hate to have to cauterize your drippin' pecker with a hot bowie knife!"

"No, you wouldn't!" Crockett returned, tipping the gang leader's hat over his eyes as he passed.

When the older man had gone inside, where the others were whooping like maverick studs in the springtime, Cannady turned to Burdette. "Let's have a drink and talk it out. I want to know everything we got ahead of us in Sundance."

"I already had enough to fill the steamer on one o' them iron train engines," said the tall Burdette, who looked more like a drover than a desperado, "but it wouldn't be polite to make you drink alone."

Inside, they ordered drinks at the bar — behind which two enchanting, eye-batting blondes dressed all in black were filling orders and parrying the drunken propositions of the miners and prospectors and Cannady's gang of newcomers. The place was dark, lit by red or blue bracket lamps and coal-oil lanterns hanging from posts. Dark, smoke-shrouded shadows slid this way and that.

There were several open, cavelike rooms, all filled with intimate nooks and crannies, some of which were hidden behind curtained doors, with tables, chairs, and benches scattered everywhere. It took Cannady and Burdette a good five minutes to find a free table — and one that wasn't missing a leg — near a doorway covered with a flour-sack curtain behind which Ed Brown was trying to convince a girl with a high voice that her rates were too steep. Over their heads angled a broad, open staircase. Men and working girls moved, hand in hand and staggeringly drunk, in a near-steady stream.

"What's this about Willie and Alfred sportin' badges?" Cannady asked, raising his voice to be heard above the din.

Burdette threw back his tequila shot, then took a long drink from his beer mug. "The sheriff o' Sundance is an old mossy-horn. Dangerous son of a bitch, I heard tell. Burt Nielsen's his name. Used to be a hide hunter and a market hunter for the railroad. Anyway, Case got wind that the man was advertisin' fer deputies. Case got this wild hair up his ass to send Willie and Alfred up there to apply. Hell, they done deputied before, you know." Burdette slapped the table and laughed. "Sure enough, they got the jobs! Our asses are covered."

Cannady threw back one of his two whiskey shots and slowly set the glass on the table, studying on what he'd just been told. He nodded slowly. "They'll get the drop on the sheriff and any other deputies, so we'll only have to worry about any heroes on the street."

"And guards from the mine," Burdette said, licking beer foam from his giant, drooping mustache. "The way Case figured it, we'll hit the bank as the loot's bein' transferred to this big, steel-frame wagon they been usin' to haul the gold down the mountains to Camp Collins in the eastern foothills. That's easiest. If we wait till the gold's in that wagon, which is more or less a big goddamn bank vault on wheels, we'll need a ton of Giant black powder to get to it . . . and probably blow ourselves to smithereens."

"Still gonna hit on Saturday?"

Burdette shook his head. "Next Tuesday. Full week. They keep changin' the schedule. That's another good reason to have Willie and Alfred workin' the inside. They're privy to every schedule change as soon as it's made. They and the sheriff and the two other deputies will be helpin' the mine guards make the transfer from the bank to the hell wagon."

"Hell wagon?"

"That's what that big steel wagon's come to be called by our fellow long riders," said Burdette with a chuckle. "Because once that gold's inside, it might as well be in hell for all the good it's gonna do anybody tryin' to get it out."

"Clayton Cannady, you son of a bitch!"

Cannady turned his head. A handsome, medium-tall gent was walking toward him, a tan duster flapping about his whipcord trousers and revealing a pearl-gripped Colt in a shoulder holster. Case Oddfellow smiled, showing a full set of perfect white teeth, a raven's wing of wavy hair flopping across his forehead. He moseyed up and stuck his hand out to Cannady.

"Had a French lesson yet?" he shouted above the unceasing noise. "They do 'em good around here!"

"Not yet," Cannady said. "But since Karl's done filled me in on Sundance, I reckon —"

Two pistol pops sounded somewhere above Cannady's head. A girl screamed — a long, shrill, bewitching exclamation of gut-wrenching terror.

The whorehouse din softened only slightly.

The pistol popped two more times, and a man shouted. The words were badly garbled, as if the man was yelling around a mouthful of rocks.

Cannady made out the words "Fuckin' bitch whore, I'll see you in holy hell!"

The din died to a low murmur.

"Shit," Cannady said, standing heavily after the hard ride and his two whiskey shots. "Think I recognize that voice."

He hitched up his gun belt, cursed again, and made for the stairs.

9

As Cannady climbed the stairs, the girl screamed again. Again, the pistol barked, and the bullet clanged sharply off metal.

Cannady chuckled dryly and hurried his pace. Nothing like shootin' up a whorehouse to draw attention to the whole gang.

Several half-clad men and girls were standing around the second-story hall, casting agitated glances at the closed, plankboard door at the hall's far end. The hall was so dark, lit only by flickering lamplight angling through a couple of open doors to the right and left, that Cannady didn't see Ed Brown till he'd nearly passed the man.

"Sounds like Paxton." Naked save for his feathered black hat, Brown wheezed a soft laugh. "Let me know if ye need any help." He turned back into the room, in which Cannady glimpsed a pair of naked female legs and a woman's bare ass on a bed, and closed the door behind him.

Cannady stopped at the door behind which the shots had been fired. Now only soft whimpers sounded, like those of a small dog, and a wooden scratching, as if rats were chewing the curtains.

Cannady tapped the door. "Paxton, what the fuck is goin' on in there, boy? You tryin' to alert Judge Bean over to Fort Smith?"

Paxton sobbed. There was a wooden thump and another scratch. Cannady drew his pistol, threw the door open, and peered into the shadows cast by a single candle flickering in a shot glass. Naked, Paxton knelt on the other side of the small room, his left cheek pressed to a stout wooden cabinet.

His chest rose and fell sharply. Sweat shone on his pale back. His right arm was covered with blood. So was his cheek and shoulder, Cannady saw as his eyes adjusted. He also saw the hilt and handle of the knife protruding from Paxton's face. Apparently, the blade had gone through Paxton's face, pinning his head to the bureau.

One of Paxton's Colt Navies lay in a spray of blood near his right foot, not far from a wooden water bucket, a bedsheet that had been twisted, soaked, and knotted into a deadly whip, and strewn clothes.

His face carved with incredulity, Cannady

stepped into the room. He stopped when Paxton, grunting and cursing, lifted his second Navy in his left hand, then, keeping his left cheek pressed snug against the cabinet, extended the gun toward the bed and fired.

Though he'd seen it coming, Cannady jumped at the loud report, his nostrils peppered with powder smoke.

"Paxton, ye crazy —"

Candlelight flickered off the smooth, obsidian handle of the knife embedded in Paxton's right jaw. Every movement evoked a cry or a muffled curse or both.

Again, Paxton fired toward the bed, the bullet sparking off the brass frame and embedding itself in the wall beyond with a crisp smack. Cannady heard the girl's sobs, but he couldn't see her. Probably under the bed.

"Christ!"

The outlaw leader moved forward, grabbed Paxton's pistol as the man raised it once more, jerked it from his hand, and flung it against the far wall. He took his own pistol in his left hand, wrapped his right hand around the knife's black handle, and gave it a jerk. It wouldn't come.

Paxton slapped a hand to the cabinet and bellowed like a poleaxed bull.

Reasserting his grip on the knife's handle, Cannady propped his left boot against the cabinet and pulled again.

Paxton's scream seared Cannady's eardrums as the knife sprang free of wood and flesh in a blood spray. Paxton fell back against the armoire, arms flapping like a crazed bird's wings, eyelids fluttering before staying closed.

His head slumped to the floor, and he lay still.

Cannady inspected the bloody knife. He'd never seen a handle so black. Some wood he'd never seen. The blade was long, thin, and serrated, the very tip hooked to make removal not only excruciating but deadly.

"Shit," Cannady grunted, bemused.

He became aware of breathing and shuffling behind him, and turned to the door. Several half-clad gang members were peering into the room, keeping their feet planted in the hall as if afraid to enter a werewolf's den.

Cannady canted his head toward Paxton. "Tend him." He turned to the bed. His dark gums and brown teeth shone between his spread lips as he grabbed the bed frame, pulled it brusquely out from the wall, and aimed his pistol at the gap.

The girl cowered on her knees, head in

her hands. Feeling the bed pulled away, she jerked her head up, her pale, oval face horrified, cheeks slick with tears.

"Come on, honey," Cannady said, depressing his pistol's hammer and dropping the gun in its sheath. He bent down, grabbed the girl's arm, and slung her over his shoulder as if she weighed little more than a feather pillow. She shuddered and made a keening sound as he headed for the door.

"You deserve a man like yourself," Cannady said, pushing into the hall. "And you done found him."

An hour after sunup the next morning, Cuno Massey and Serenity Parker rode into a small, unnamed crossroads settlement situated in the V between two sun-dappled creeks. The sounds of picks and chisels hammering rock rose from the upper slopes, and an occasional dynamite blast echoed, scaring waxwings from the pine trees.

A young bearded man in a flat-brimmed, low-crowned leather hat and high, laced boots stood knee-deep in the southern fork, swirling a partly submerged pan while a golden retriever splashed from bank to bank, chasing invisible ducks.

As Massey steered his wagon toward the

chinked-log blacksmith barn on their right, loud voices rose from the big canvas and wood structure, a board shingle announcing MERCANTILE, on their left. The mercantile's double doors burst open and four big men in long coats appeared on the broad front stoop, carrying a small, round-faced, black-haired gent between them like a battering ram.

The four saddle horses tied to the hitch rack gave a start, sidling away, as the four men swung the diminutive gent forward and back, counting the swings.

"Five!"

They catapulted the little gent a good fifteen feet straight out from the boardwalk, his body a blur as it arced over the street before Cuno's wagon. It plopped belly-down in mud left by a passing shower.

There was no splash. Just a dull, wet plop.

"Like Wild Dan said," shouted one of the throwers, black-bearded, pale-skinned, and wearing a broad-brimmed Stetson, "no Chinks allowed!"

Laughing, he and the other three wheeled and walked back into the mercantile. The doors stood wide behind them. The chimney pipe poking from the roof sent blue smoke flattening out over the dirty canvas and tinging the air with pine.

Cuno stopped his mules fifteen feet from the short, slender man lying belly-down in the mud. The man lifted his round, mud-smeared face, spat filth from his lips. He raised an arm to clean his face, only smearing it. Finally, he pushed himself onto his knees. As he looked around through enraged eyes, his gaze landed on Cuno and Serenity.

"Why you stare?" he growled in a heavy Chinese accent. He raised his small, pale fists. "I in way? Go 'round! Get the hell outta my sight, or I climb up and beat the hell outta you both!"

Cuno held the man's gaze for a moment, glanced again at the mercantile, then gigged the mule forward, swinging wide of the Chinaman and stopping before the blacksmith barn. He set the break and dropped over the wheel, landing flat-footed.

"Have the smithy tend that rim and tar the axle," he told Serenity. Without waiting for a reply, he strode over to where the Chinamen knelt in the mud.

"Gosh darn," Serenity said, rubbing a nervous hand across his beard. "It's awful early fer trouble . . ."

As Serenity sidled around the mule, heading for the barn's open door while casting nervous glances at Cuno, Cuno crouched beside the Chinaman.

The man was rubbing a sleeve of his black, wool coat across his face. Lowering the arm, he saw Cuno, and jerked with a start. Cuno extended a clean, red handkerchief. The man looked at it, his black eyes gaining a wary cast as they returned to Cuno's.

The freighter canted his head toward the mercantile. "What do you need?"

Skeptically, as if expecting the handkerchief to be snapped away, he pinched the dangling cloth between two fingers green-caked with fresh horse shit. "Tea, flour. Rope."

Cuno stood and began moving toward the mercantile.

"Monkshood tea."

Cuno stopped, turned.

"Some ground wheat and beans," the Chinaman added somberly, bowing his head. "And a little molasses . . . for sweet."

Cuno snorted, turned, and mounted the mercantile's broad stoop, glanced at the live chickens hunkered in cages stacked left of the door. A sign over one of the cages read: RHODE ISLAND REDS — $1. Passing through the open doors, Cuno slung his gaze around the broad tent lined with overflowing shelves on two sides and packed with crates and barrels. A long counter

121

stood to his right.

Near the smoky stove in the far left corner, the four bearded men played Red Dog atop a nail keg, hats shoved back on their heads. The man whom Cuno took to be the leader sat his chair backward, resting a brawny arm on the back and berating one of his brethren for betting too low. He wore a long braid down his back, Indian style, though he was definitely a white man.

The air smelled of tobacco smoke, moldy canvas, and the assorted dry goods straining the whipsawed pine shelves.

As Cuno looked around, a portly, clean-shaven gent in soiled duck trousers and a black opera hat entered through the back door with an armload of split pine logs. He gave Cuno a bored glance, dumped the wood into the crate beside the stove, then sauntered behind the counter. He stopped across from Cuno, who was eyeing the new repeaters racked beside a Cuckoo clock trimmed with a placard that promised, MADE IN SWITSERLAND!

"What'll it be, mister?" the big gent said with a tired sigh.

"Rope, molasses, wheat, beans, and tea. Monkshood tea. On a separate ticket, put a bag of Arbuckles, bottle of whiskey, ten pounds of oats, four boxes of forty-four shells, one of forty-fives."

The man's dull blue eyes sharpened suspiciously as he studied Cuno from beneath the brim of the shabby opera hat, the crown of which was decorated with a single, long, curved tooth of a grizzly bear. Cuno held the man's gaze with a mild one of his own. Behind him and left, the four bearded gents stopped bickering. Cuno felt their eyes on his back.

The portly gent behind the counter slid a quick glance at the others, then slowly turned to begin filling the order.

A man behind Cuno grunted, "Monkshood tea." A slight pause. "Ain't that what that slanty-eyed heathen ordered?"

Cuno kept his back to the man, fists on the countertop. top. "That's what he ordered."

The portly clerk stopped dipping molasses into a jar to regard Cuno gravely, then slid his eyes to the rear of the room. At length, he continued filling Cuno's order.

Cuno looked into a sack of hard candy, perused a box of miners' denim. He'd picked up a hobnailed boot and was inspecting the heel when a chair scraped across the hard-packed floor.

Boots scuffed toward him. The big gent with the braid appeared to Cuno's left, bending over the counter to get a look at his face.

"You buyin' tea fer that Chink?" The man curled his upper lip. "Who the hell you think you are?"

Cuno set the boot down and turned to the man, whose brown eyes flashed angry little darts. "Name's Massey, and I'll buy tea or anything else for anyone I like."

The clerk set a small burlap bag on the counter. "That's the tea an' such," he grumbled.

The bearded gent with the braid kept his eyes on Cuno, but addressed the clerk. "Put it back, Roy."

Roy's lips moved, but he didn't say anything as he shuttled his tentative glance between Massey and the hard case with the braid.

"Total it up," Cuno told him.

The hard case stretched a disbelieving smile and hitched an elbow on the counter. He cast a glance at the back of the room, where the other three men had fallen silent, then returned his mocking gaze to Cuno.

"Young man, what'd I just tell you? Roy here has a policy against servin' heathen furriners."

Cuno kept his eyes on the hard case, but addressed Roy. "Total it up and start fillin' the other order."

The hard case chuffed and dropped his head sharply, as if he couldn't believe the stupidity of this tinhorn.

The men at the back of the tent chuckled. "Maybe he's foreign his ownself and needs an English lesson," said one.

A chair scraped back, and the man nearest the stove, wearing a deerskin cloak around his shoulders, said, "Maybe he needs the same English lesson we gave the Chink."

"I don't know," said the man nearest Cuno, staring at the others, chuckling. "Maybe he just needs his ears cleaned out. And you know me, boys. I got just the thing."

He wheeled toward Cuno, swinging his right fist. Cuno raised his left hand, palm out.

The hard case's fist smacked into it as if against a stone wall. The hard case's eyes narrowed in shock. Cuno stared into them blandly as he closed his fingers over the hard case's fist, snapped the man's hand back sharply.

The bones in the man's fist snapped like kindling.

"*Ahhhh!*" the man roared, watching his hand dangling like a scrap of burlap, cracked bones showing through the hairy wrist. He dropped to his knees, face balled with pain, while he cursed and jabbed his left hand across his waist for the Colt Lightning holstered on his right hip.

Before the hard case could fumble the gun from the holster, Cuno stepped forward and brought his right knee up under the man's chin. There was a sharp clack of shattering teeth.

The man's head snapped back. Giving a clipped groan, he hit the floor on his back, spitting bits of broken teeth as his eyes fluttered closed. He lay still, the look of excruciating pain slitting his eyes and dimpling his cheeks.

"Jee-*sus!*" exclaimed the clerk, glancing over the counter at the fallen hard case.

To Cuno's left, another chair scraped back. Curses and the thunder of boot heels echoed. Cuno grabbed his .44 and, thumbing the hammer back, turned to aim the gun at the other three hard cases scrambling toward him.

Seeing the gun, they all froze in unison, hands on their own sheathed pistols.

The man with the deerskin cloak was closest to Cuno. He shifted his gaze from his fallen partner to the freighter, gritting his teeth. "You son of a bitch."

Cuno angled the pistol barrel down. *Pop!* The slug drilled a ragged hole through the soft toe of the hard case's boot. He cursed and hopped on his other foot.

"Owww! Goddamn, you son of a *sow!"*

Cuno raised the pistol again, hammer cocked. While keeping the gun aimed at the three hard cases glaring at him from twelve feet away, Cuno addressed the clerk. "Any law around here?"

Lower jaw hanging, the clerk shook his head.

Cuno grunted and swept his gaze around the three standing hard cases. The one with the wounded foot stood on his good one, holding his other foot above the ground. Blood dribbled from the ragged hole in the toe, seeping into the hard-packed dirt.

"If you get a hankerin' to trail me, just remember there's more where this came from."

He canted his head slightly toward the clerk. "Finish my order and tally it."

While the clerk scrambled around behind the counter, then scuttled over to the oat bin near the smoking stove, Cuno glared at the three hard cases. He pointed his gun at the small square table about five feet to his left, where an empty bottle and shot glass sat. A cigar stub lay at the bottom of the glass.

"You boys set your pistol belts on that table, then back up to your own table and sit down."

Reluctantly, still cursing under their breath and sliding skeptical glances at their fallen comrade, out like a blown wick, blood trickling out both corners of his mouth, they did as they'd been told. When they were all seated at their table, the clerk set Cuno's two sacks on the counter, and gave him the total for each order.

Cuno flipped several coins to the man, who caught them against his chest. The freighter grabbed the sacks by their necks, and threw them over his left shoulder. Keeping his cocked pistol aimed at the three hard cases sitting their chairs in the far rear corner, scowling at him, hands in their laps, he backed toward the door.

"Poke your noses out this door before I leave town, and I'll blow 'em off."

With that, he turned and went out.

He angled across the rutted trail toward his wagon parked before the blacksmith shop, which was gushing black smoke from its chimney pipe. Serenity Parker and the blacksmith had the right front wheel off and leaning against the jacked-up wagon. They stood side by side, staring toward the mercantile with wary casts to their eyes.

The Chinaman sat on a pine stump left of the shop, under a wind-buffeted aspen. He'd cleaned his face. His wool coat lay across his lap, and he scrubbed at it with a rag.

Cuno walked over to the man, dropped the bag in his lap. "Came to a dollar forty-nine."

The Chinaman stared down at the bag, placed a hand on it to make sure it was really there. He lifted his chin toward Cuno, upper lip curled with disbelief. As if jolted from a dream, he stood and stuck his right hand into a pocket of his dirty cotton trousers, pulled out several lint-peppered coins, and dropped them in Cuno's Gloved palm.

Cuno closed his fingers over the coins and nodded. "I wouldn't hang around here long. Your friends are a mite piss-burned."

He pinched his hat brim at the Chinaman, turned, and strode off toward the wagon.

10

When the wagon had been repaired, Cuno and Serenity Parker followed the curving wagon trail up out of the valley and into the high spruce parks, where the creeks were narrow and swift and the air was a good ten degrees colder than down below.

Steel-blue rain clouds gathered after midday. As the wagon climbed higher, the rain turned to snow. There was little wind and the temperature didn't drop much below thirty, so there was no danger of exposure or blocked roads. The day ended early, however, the soft gray light dimming as though a giant lamp was turned down.

Cuno parked beside the south fork of Roaring Creek, just upriver from an old Ute burial scaffold from which old buckskins and beaded blankets hung like tattered ribbons, revealing what the hawks and eagles had left of the Indians' bleached bones.

Clad in a long duck coat and ancient

Confederate cavalry hat, a red muffler wrapped around his scrawny neck, Serenity gathered wood for a fire while Cuno picketed the mules in the high bluestem by the creek. Cuno had removed his camping gear from the wagon box, along with the fresh Arbuckles, when a shadow flicked through the trees on the other side of the trail. He stopped, turned his head that way, breathing slowly through his mouth to listen.

Above the sound of the sifting snow and Serenity's wheezing and scuffling, weeds cracked softly, the falling snow somehow softening and clarifying even the slightest sounds. Snow crunched under small hooves — the double thuds of a mule deer bounding away from suspected danger.

Cuno walked to the front of the wagon, grabbed his Winchester from the driver's box, and glanced at Serenity, who'd just dropped a load of kindling near an old fire ring. "Be back in a bit."

The old man — a scrawny, scarved, bearded visage in the failing light and slanting snow — turned toward him. "Where you off to?"

Cuno rammed a fresh round into the Winchester's breech and started across the trail to the aspen-stippled hill rising on the other side. "Meat."

"I heard it," Serenity said, breathing hard, his phlegmy voice clear in the still air. "Didn't think you did. Got good ears on ye, fer a pup."

The old man chuckled softly and cracked a stick over his scrawny knee. Cuno climbed the low bank. He slanted through the aspens, finding a freshly rubbed sapling with bark bits littering the snow at its base. In the grainy snow only partially covering the fallen leaves were hoofprints and fresh urine dribbles. A buck then. A small one, judging by the size of the hoofprints. Cuno probably outweighed him. The deer had lost a tip off one of its front toes.

Cuno hefted the Winchester in his hands and continued up the bank. He left the trees behind and crossed a small clearing, the ground still pitching up on his right, toward a crest of scattered boulders and cedars barely seen through pines and the snow fog.

He descended a wooded trough in which a narrow, black freshet trickled amidst ice-crusted stones, and clambered up the other side. His boots slipped and slid in the slick, wet leaves and snow-mashed bluestem. He fell once, felt the icy sting of snow under his sleeve, then pushed quietly through some shagbush and into another clearing.

He stopped, slowly raised the Winchester.

Forty yards ahead, the buck stood nibbling leaves from a chokecherry shrub, jerking its head to rip the foliage from the limbs. A little buck with a big set of antlers. Cuno did outweigh him. The buck chewed, stopped, looked around, then began chewing again.

Cuno dropped to a knee and raised the rifle to his shoulder. He thumbed the hammer back, planted a bead on the animal's left front shoulder, then brought it back and up slightly. Cuno took a deep breath, held it, and began taking up the trigger slack.

The buck jerked suddenly, flinched, twisted slightly, moved forward several steps, froze, and dropped — a dun heap upon the white-dusted grass.

Cuno's eyes widened. He relaxed his trigger finger but kept the rifle snugged to his cheek as he looked around the clearing.

Heart beating rhythmically, his curiosity getting the better of him — deer didn't suddenly collapse when you were drawing a bead on them — he lowered the Winchester slightly but kept the hammer cocked. Carrying the rifle across his chest, swinging his wary gaze from left to right and back again, he made his way across the clearing. He winced at the crunch and rustle of his boots.

No movement to either side or behind.

Just the slow, occasional breeze gusts nudging snow tufts from wet branches. A small cottontail scuttled through the snow to his left, disappeared in the brush.

Cuno approached the deer and stopped, looked down. The animal's eyes were glassy. Blood splotched the snow around its snout and soaked the fir over its right shoulder, around the four inches of feathered arrow protruding from its side.

Cuno crouched and again swept the clearing with his gaze. The shot had to have come from the buck's right. Cuno stared in that direction, but kept his rifle down by his knee.

He'd let the brave fetch his deer. He'd earned it. Cuno wanted no trouble with Indians. He couldn't just walk away, though. The shooter of that arrow was no doubt watching him from the evergreens on the other side of the clearing. You gave an Indian no reason to believe you weak-hearted. When the man showed himself, Cuno would give a curt nod to indicate his surrender of the other man's meat. Only then would he walk away.

When he'd crouched there for a couple of minutes, and nothing happened, he grabbed the end of the arrow, pulled it out of the deer. Blood dribbled from the strap-iron blade. The shaft was slender, painted black with pitch, and fletched with falcon feathers.

Something sharp prodded his back, pushing through his coat. He leapt forward and swung around, dropping the arrow and bringing the Winchester up. His assailant shuffled nimbly back and raised the nocked arrow as if to show Cuno what had prodded him.

The man standing before Cuno was short, thin, and bowlegged, with a dozen or so fine, black hairs drooping off his chin. He wore a deerskin hat with dangling ear-flaps, quilted hide coat, baggy duck trousers, and knee-high, fur-trimmed mocassins. He wasn't wearing gloves. The short bow he held in his stubby, brown hands was made of ash wood and sinew, with rabbit fur wrapped around each end to muffle the twang of the shot.

The man's deerskin hat rose to a peak, giving him an odd, gremlinlike appearance.

As Cuno stared, holding the Winchester taut but only chest-high, the barrel canted sensibly askance, the man let the bowstring creak back toward the bow. The nocked arrow sagged. White teeth shone within the dark circle of the hat. The man reached up with one hand, removed the hat from his head, lowered it to his side. As his smile grew wider, showing more small, square teeth, the outside corners of his slanted eyes drew up toward his temples.

The Chinaman from the mercantile.

Cuno grunted. "I'll be damned."

"You want meat?" The man's voice was husky and deep. "You take."

Cuno stared at the bow and the arrow, his curiosity about how the man had gotten his hands on such implements tempered with annoyance at having the meat shot out from under him. He glanced at the deer and shook his head. "It's yours."

Cuno rested the Winchester over his shoulder and walked back the way he'd come.

Later that night, the snow stopped and the sky cleared, leaving high wisps of clouds smearing the light of a half-moon and dimming the stars. The air was damp and cold. The creek gurgled over the rocks. The fire felt good as Cuno and Parker, hunkered down in their heavy coats, washed their beans and biscuits down with strong, hot coffee.

"That's the problem with you young colts, you're slicker'n snot with a hogleg, but ye ain't worth spit with a long gun."

Cuno was about to respond when he lifted his head suddenly. Quietly, he set his plate and fork on a rock in the fire ring and grabbed the Winchester leaning beside him. He snapped a shell into the breech. Parker snapped his eyes up and threw up a hand, palm out, beans dribbling into his beard.

"I was just joshin', son!"

"Quiet," Cuno admonished, expressionless, staring over the oldster's right shoulder. He raised his voice. "Come in slow."

Silence except for the fire's snaps and breathy gutter. Parker craned his head to follow Cuno's gaze into the shadows near the wagon. Behind Cuno, one of the mules brayed.

A diminutive figure materialized from the shadows — a small, bandy-legged man with a peaked hat and dangling earflaps. The Chinaman moved slowly into the firelight, the flames bringing out the pale yellow of his face. He bowed his head repeatedly, a cautious cast to his gaze. He carried some kind of pack on his back. The short bow was slung over one shoulder, and feathered arrows from the quiver poked up from behind one shoulder.

"I bring meat. We share, huh?" He shrugged the heavy pack off his shoulder. Not a pack, but the rolled hide of the little buck he'd shot, secured with rawhide straps. "Meat for fire?"

Cuno depressed the Winchester's trigger, leaned the rifle against the log beside him. He glanced at Parker. "Why not?"

The Chinaman shuttled his gaze between them, grinning, then dropped to his knees, setting the rolled hide on the ground before the fire. He untied the rawhide straps securing the bundle, and flipped out the corners, revealing the dark meat expertly carved, several small roasts tied with sinew. Nothing had gone to waste. The heart, lungs, liver, tongue, and even the gall bladder were there, gleaming succulently in the fire's umber glow.

"Would you look at that?" Parker rubbed his hands together. "That looks good 'nough to eat raw!"

"We no eat raw." The Chinaman set his bow and arrows against the log on which Cuno sat, and stood. Sliding a knife from a sheath beneath his quilted coat, he scuttled off into the darkness.

Sipping their coffee, Cuno and Parker listened to the man thrashing around in the pines, trampling brush and snapping branches. The night was so quiet that they could hear his industrious grunts and sighs above the creek's relentless murmur.

A few minutes later, he shuffled back into the firelight. He carried two long aspen sticks under one arm. In his hands he was sharpening another long stick with a wide-bladed, bone-handled knife.

When he had a good point on the stick, he knelt before the venison chunks, picked through the roasts, then skewered a fist-sized hunk of tenderloin onto the stick he'd just sharpened. Smiling and bowing, he handed the stick to Cuno, breathing sharply and making soft, satisfied sounds through his parted lips. His thin, stringy chin whiskers brushed his chest.

Cuno took the stick. "Obliged." He held the roast over the fire.

The Chinaman sharpened another stick, skewered another fist-sized roast onto the end, and handed that stick to Parker, who'd watched the man like a hungry dog awaiting a dropped scrap. Parker accepted the stick with an eager grin, several beans still crusted in his beard, and held the meat out over the fire.

Parker shook his head, his blue eyes sparkling in the firelight. "There ain't nothin' like venison when you thought you was gonna have to hit the hay on beans!"

Cuno gave him a wry look from beneath his brows. The old man's grin faded, a contrite look taking its place as he returned his eyes to the meat beginning to smoke at the end of his stick.

When the Chinaman was roasting half the liver on his own stick, sitting Indian style before the fire, Cuno glanced at the bow and arrow leaning against the log to his left. "Well-put-together shootin' tools you got there."

The Chinaman looked at the short bow and the quiver, and chuckled huskily. "Very sharp . . . and very quiet."

"If I didn't know better," Parker said, inspecting his meat, "I'd say you was part Injun."

"I work the railroad with the son of an old Indian chief," the Chinaman said, slowly turning the stick so the liver cooked evenly. "A Cheyenne brave. He taught me to make bow and arrow, to hunt." He shook his head with gravity. "To be very quiet!"

Cuno turned his own stick and said dryly, "You learned right well."

"I am Kong."

Cuno held out his hand, and the Chinaman shook it. "Cuno Massey. The old man with the dirty beard yonder is Serenity Parker."

"You can call me Serenity," the old man said, shaking the Chinaman's hand. "What

140

brings you so far from the railroad, Mr. Kong?"

The Chinaman's eyes lost any semblance of humor as they stared at the liver browning nicely in the licking flames. "I have daughter, but my wife die. I quit railroad. It is hard life for child. I come to mountains, prospect for gold." He shook his head. "I find none, so I work in saloon. Now, saloon burn down. Bad men burn it down. Take my daughter."

Cuno turned his gaze to the Chinaman gritting his teeth as he stared angrily into the flames. "This happen recently?" the freighter asked.

Kong nodded.

"Big gang of men?" Serenity gazed at the Chinaman now too. "Call themselves The Committee?"

Scowl lines cutting deep into his forehead, Kong looked at Parker, then at Cuno. "You know these men?"

"Know *of* 'em." Cuno lifted his coffee to his lips, and sipped. "I'm gonna kill 'em."

The Chinaman furled his brows as he stared at Cuno.

"They killed his partner," Serenity explained. "Cuno an' me are on the vengeance trail."

"Vengeance trail." Kong spoke the words

slowly, then again, as if memorizing them. His voice quivered with emotion. "I know this trail."

"It's a hard one," Cuno said. "Not one you tread lightly."

"No," the Chinaman agreed, removing the liver from the fire. He set it on a rock and cut it with his knife. "But one I must tread quickly. My daughter is strong, and she will fight. They will kill her."

He slipped a chunk of liver into his mouth and, holding the skewered meat in his other hand, gained his feet. With his free hand, he reached down and slung his quiver over his shoulder, then his bow.

Serenity stared up at him, aghast. "You ain't headin' off again already, are ya?"

Kong tore off another chunk of meat and chewed hungrily. "I must keep moving. Must catch up with my daughter." He squatted down, stuffed his coat pockets with meat chunks, and straightened. "Rest of meat yours. Obliged for fire."

Cuno frowned up at him. "This vengeance trail ain't to be taken light, or too fast. Especially when you're only armed with a bow and arrow."

"No time waste!"

"You best bed down here tonight," Serenity urged. "You can ride out with us in the mornin'. Hell, we're all after the same gang."

"No time waste," Kong insisted as he scrambled back off the way he'd come. He stopped and turned back, bowing. "For fire, cooked meat . . . much 'bliged!"

Then he was gone.

When his footsteps had dwindled, and there was only the crackling of the fire and the constant, hollow rush of the stream, Serenity looked at Cuno.

He shook his head and bit off a chunk of meat from his stick. "That's one crazy Chinaman."

11

Early the next morning, Serenity Parker lifted his head from the balled burlap he used for a pillow, and peered out from beneath the freight wagon. A wooden cracking and heavy, regular breathing sounded on the other side of the fire in which the coffeepot chugged and gurgled.

Serenity blinked as if to clear his vision, and stared through dawn's milky, shadowy wash where the still, damp air was scented with pine smoke and fresh coffee.

On the other side of the fire, Cuno Massey hung by both hands from a low pine branch, his boots dangling a foot above the ground. The burly, young freighter was naked from the waist up. As he pulled himself toward the branch, the heavy muscles bunched and balled in his arms and shoulders, drawing the slablike pectorals up toward his neck.

His face was red, veins forking above the

bridge of his nose.

When his chin grazed the branch, he lowered himself slowly, until his arms stretched straight above his shoulders, his boot heels brushing the ground. He sucked a deep breath through his teeth and hoisted himself back up toward the branch.

Parker blinked again, ran a hand across his mouth. "What in the name o' God's got into you?"

Massey brushed his chin against the branch three more times, then dropped, boots hitting the ground with a single, solid clomp. He brushed his hands together, and grabbed his shirt and hat from a mossy boulder.

"Just keepin' in shape for mule wrestlin'. Come on, old man. Time to get up. Coffee's done and the sun's nearly up."

"You've gone ape on me, boy. Sure 'nough."

"My pa taught me that exercise — a pull-up they call it — when I wrestled and boxed for extra money summers back home. If you're good, maybe I'll teach you."

"I ain't no hairy-assed ape like some!"

Cuno reached under the wagon, pulled out his bedroll and the saddlebags he'd used for a pillow. Tossing both into the wagon box, he prodded the old man with a boot toe. "Come on, Serenity. If I'd known you were gonna lay around all mornin' like Jay Gould, I'd have sent you home when I first spied your mangy carcass falling off my tailgate."

Serenity rolled over and threw his blanket over his old, gray head. "It's too early and my ole bones are chilled."

When Cuno spitted some of the venison over the fire, and the fumes wafted over the wagon, the old man rolled out of his soogan, working his nose and smacking his lips. In a few minutes, he'd tugged his boots on and crawled out from beneath the big Murphy, wrapping a blanket over his shoulders and hitching up his pants.

"Ah." He grinned, clapping his butternut-gray hat on his head. "Always did like the smell of venison on a cold autumn morn."

An hour later, the sun was up and the snow was all but melted off, leaving light mud and occasional fog wisps in its wake. The fog was especially thick over the creek, which they hugged on their right, rising up like steam from a slow-boiling river.

The mules were clomping smartly along a flat, making good time, and Serenity was singing an old Southern hymn, when pistol and rifle fire snapped on the other side of the creek.

Cuno hauled back on the mules' reins. Serenity stopped singing and turned his head to the right, furling his bushy brows.

"What the hell you s'pose that's about?"

Cuno stared across the creek, toward a low, pine-covered rise about a half mile ahead. Two more shots sounded, then two more.

Could be hunters, but somehow the shots sounded angry. Like men shooting at men. Not likely to be Committee members, but they might as well check it out.

Cuno slapped the reins across the mules' backs. As the team trotted out, Serenity reached under the seat for his double-bore, and broke it open, making sure both barrels were loaded with wads.

Hearing several more shots, they rode for a half mile before crossing the creek at a rocky ford and mounting the northern bank spotted with wild currant and shagbush. Cows began to appear, a few skinny heifers and one-year-old steers overgrazing the stream banks. Probably a settlement near. Gradually, angry voices rose from dead ahead.

Gaining a shady cottonwood copse, Cuno stopped the team and sat listening. The voices seemed to originate from the other side of the trees.

He wrapped the reins around the brake handle, grabbed his Winchester, and leapt to the ground. "Stay with the wagon."

Cuno jacked a round into the Winchester's chamber, off-cocked the hammer, and jogged through the trees, angling toward the direction of the rising din. One man seemed to be doing most of the yelling. A pistol spoke intermittently — a .36-caliber, judging by the report.

Once past the trees, Cuno bounded up a low hill pocked with rocks, piñon pines, and junipers. Near the crest, he swiped his hat from his head, hunkered down beside a square hunk of sandstone, which had probably tumbled off the northern ridge, and peered down the other side of the hill.

A makeshift tent camp — with a few a plank shacks and the usual smelly privies and trash heaps and scrounging mutts — stretched across the flat beyond the hill's base. Cattle cropped the tough, brown grass around the camp's perimeter, having already ravaged the creek bank.

The little settlement was deserted at the moment. Probably every prospector who called the place home had gathered at a tall cottonwood on Cuno's side of the village, fifty yards from the hill's base.

The crowd of fifteen to twenty men milled

in a close group. Several carried rifles. A few wore pistols strapped to their hips. One man triggered shots into the air while whooping loudly, as though to keep the gang's blood surging. Others carried shovels or hickory ax handles.

Cuno dropped his right knee to the ground, and swept a lock of sandy-blond hair from his right eye. Most likely a shovel fight. Miners liked nothing more than to bash one another's skulls in with shovels. If they were really pissed and really drunk, they'd sling pickaxes.

On his last trip, Cuno had seen what was left after a pick fight. Until he was told better, he'd assumed a hog had been butchered.

Cuno was about to straighten up and head back to the wagon, when the crowd shifted curiously. The center opened slightly, and two men in hats led another, bare-headed man toward the sprawling cottonwood. Cuno stayed hunkered down, staring into the crowd, holding the Winchester across his thighs.

The man with the pistol must have emptied his cylinder, because the gun had fallen silent. The crowd roared louder, as if to make up for the lack of pistol fire. Barking dogs ran amidst the prospectors, and two young boys on a horse watched from the village side of the meadow. A rope was thrown over a branch of the cottonwood. Several men milled around the base of the tree.

Suddenly, the crowd opened around the bare-headed man, shouting even more loudly than before. The bare-headed man suddenly rose straight up toward the branch above, kicking and clawing at the rope around his neck, jerking this way and that. Short-cropped black hair capped a round face. He wore baggy duck trousers and fur-trimmed moccasins.

Cuno's heart thudded. Kong.

The crowd whooped and clapped.

Someone shouted, "Let the heathen suffocate!"

"Teach him to steal *my* mule!" yelled another.

Cuno took several quick, deep breaths as he snapped the rifle to his shoulder. He let out a long breath, held it, aimed, and squeezed the rifle's trigger.

The Winchester jumped and barked. Cuno stared through the billowing powder smoke as the slug smacked into the cottonwood's trunk, spraying bark.

Quickly, Cuno levered another shell, aimed, and fired.

The slug sliced the rope above Kong's head cleanly. The Chinaman dropped, disappeared amidst the crowd, most of whom had jerked around to stare in the direction from which the shot had come.

Cuno pushed himself to his feet and, ejecting the spent shell, held the rifle straight out from his hip in one hand as he strode down the hill. He slid the barrel around the crowd, threatening, and slitted his eyes beneath the shading brim of his hat.

The man who seemed to be the necktie party's leader stepped forward — a short, pudgy man with a thin red beard and floppy-brimmed green hat. He wore an old Civil War model pistol on his hip. "Who the hell're *you?*"

Cuno paused about twenty feet from the crowd, kept his rifle butt snugged against his belt, its hammer at full cock. "I'm the Chinaman's guardian angel." He lifted his head to see into the crowd. "Kong?"

A grunt sounded. The crowd parted as the Chinaman bolted through it, heading toward Cuno, his black-haired head bobbing around most of the other's men's shoulders. When he surfaced, he ran past the leader, who promptly stuck his right boot out. Kong's left ankle hit the boot and, hands tied behind his back, the Chinaman

151

fell headlong into the sand and sage.

The leader stepped forward, turned sideways, and poked an angry finger at Cuno. "That son-of-fuckin' Han tried to steal my mule! Now, in a minin' camp, the law for horse thievin' or mule thievin' —"

"Or any kind of thievin'!" shouted someone from the crowd.

"Or *any* kind of thievin'," agreed the leader, nodding, "is *hangin'.* You got no right to interfere!"

A wagon clattered along the trail to Cuno's left. He turned a quick glance. Serenity Parker had pulled the wagon up to the edge of the meadow, the two-bore resting across the oldster's thighs. He hauled back on the reins, stopping the mules, and sat scowling toward the crowd.

Cuno turned back to the leader, canted his head toward the Chinaman, whose eyes were swelling, blood trickling from his cracked and swollen lips.

"His daughter was kidnapped," Cuno said mildly. "I'm sure he'd have returned the mule when he got her back. Wouldn't you have, Kong?"

The Chinaman had gained his knees and was glancing around anxiously. He looked at Cuno and nodded. He raised his chin toward the necktie party's leader and nodded again vigorously. "I return! I return!"

The leader scowled. "You return — bullshit!"

Cuno spied movement ahead and left. The man who'd been shooting his pistol into the air gave a drunken chuckle as he stepped out from behind another man who was holding an ax handle. The shooter flicked his old Navy toward Cuno, thumbing the hammer back.

Cuno pivoted, swinging the Winchester's barrel toward the shooter. The Winchester spoke. The shooter screamed. He dropped the Navy. Smacking the ground, the pistol discharged. The slug plunked into the ankle of another prospector, who yelled and jumped on his good foot before falling into the crowd.

The man Cuno had shot clutched his bloody forearm. *"Son of a bitch shot me!"*

Cuno lowered the Winchester's barrel slightly, triggered another shot, spraying up gravel into the man's face and knocking him back on his hands with a terrified howl.

Cuno gritted his teeth at him. "Shut up." He glanced at Kong. "Head over to the wagon. Move!"

As Kong heaved himself to his feet, the leader stared at the smoking barrel of Cuno's Winchester and stepped back, hold-

153

ing his hands chest-high in supplication. A scowl still pinched his nose, but fear had entered his eyes. He didn't say anything as Cuno backed toward the wagon, swinging the Winchester's barrel around the crowd, which had gone unnaturally quiet.

The two wounded men groaned softly. The dogs made the most noise, sniffing around and panting.

Cuno backed to within fifteen feet of the wagon, then turned. Kong sat in the driver's box beside Serenity, who was sawing through the rope tying Kong's wrists behind his back. Cuno walked around to the driver's side, climbed aboard, grabbed the reins off the brake handle, and released the brake.

He flicked the reins. As the wagon jerked forward, he appraised the crowd, the prospectors now milling and conversing in angry, albeit hushed, tones. The dogs had lost interest in the men and were chasing a rabbit up the northern ridge through the pines.

As the wagon rolled even with the two boys sitting the old, swaybacked paint bareback, the youngsters watched Cuno with keen interest.

"You a gunslinger?" asked the boy in front, swiveling his head as the wagon passed. He wore a soiled trail hat manufactured for a much older man.

Serenity cackled wickedly, jerked a thumb at Cuno. "He'll shoot ye dead and turn ye inside out, boys!" The old man threw his head back on his shoulders and roared.

Sobering, he cleared his throat and brushed a finger across his beaklike nose. "Less'n you're a deer, that is . . ."

12

"What caused you to pull such a fool stunt anyway?" Serenity asked the Chinaman when they'd ridden for a while in grim silence and they were sure the prospectors weren't trailing them.

"His daughter," Cuno said when Kong didn't answer but only stared, brooding, over the mules' twitching ears. "He thought he'd steal a mount and ride on up to The Committee, twanging away with his bow and arrow, and rip the girl right out from under 'em."

Serenity had been working a good cheek of chaw for the past forty-five minutes. Now he spat a quarter of it onto the double-tree hitch, then sat back and ran a greasy sleeve across his beard.

The air had warmed and they no longer wore coats. The only sign of last night's snow was a quicker pace to the streams they hugged as they climbed toward Sundance through fir-walled valleys.

"Good way to get her killed," Serenity said. "Good way to get yourself killed too. Me, I seen The Committee at work. Armed with just a bow and arrow, you wouldn't have a chance."

Kong stared straight ahead, the bridge of his blunt nose deeply creased. "Kong no dummy. I find Li Mei, wait for night. Go in and" — he made a snatching motion with his hand — "steal her away!"

"That might work," Cuno allowed. "It'd work better, though, to bide your time, trail the gang slow. They're heading for Sundance. Got 'em a bank to rob. No doubt, they'll split up a time or two before they get there. A gang that size never hangs together long. They get in women trouble or fighting trouble. Besides, Cannady left his brother and several other men behind. He probably expects to meet up with them again soon."

Serenity chuckled dryly.

Cuno continued. "Some'll fall back for a while, catch up to the others later. If we can knock off the stragglers, we'll have a smaller bunch to face when we finally meet Cannady in Sundance."

"They ride horses," Kong pointed out. "We may not catch up to them. They might rob and be on their way, like rabbits with a fox on their heels!"

"Maybe," Cuno said. "Comes to that, we'll rent horses in Sundance. Trail 'em from there."

"By then, Li Mei could be dead."

"That's true too," Cuno said. "A good way to make sure she's killed is to ride in like a donkey with cans tied to its tail."

"With just a bow and arrow," added Serenity.

"Take it from me." Cuno turned to Kong. "The keys to getting your daughter back are patience and relentlessness."

Kong held his gaze with a dark one of his own. "You young to know so much about manhunting."

Cuno squinted into the dust. "Yep."

They hadn't ridden much farther before a four-mule hitch and a big Cleveland dead-axle freight wagon appeared, heading toward them around a bend in the trail ahead. Cuno recognized Bull Stevens and his cousin, Lyle, sitting the driver's box, their floppy-brimmed hats flapping in the wind. By the way the wagon bounced and rattled over the ruts, Cuno knew it was empty.

Cuno reined in his own team. Bull Stevens did likewise, throwing his shoulders back and bellowing, "Hoooooo-ahhh!"

The wagons sat side by side, dust sifting,

the mules braying contentiously, stomping their feet. One of Stevens's big Arkansas blacks dropped several plops in the trail dust to Cuno's left.

Stevens grinned and slitted his good eye. He'd lost the other to the man who'd cuckolded him during the fight that left the cuckolder's throat laid wide, the man's soul sent to heaven. "That's what he thinks of you, Massey."

"Your hitch doesn't have any better manners than you do, Bull. How they hangin', Lyle?"

Lyle Stevens grimaced and cupped his crotch. "Funny you should mention 'em. Think I picked up some drip on the way up trail."

"Which whorehouse?" Serenity asked with alarm.

"Heaven's Bane."

"Aptly named," Serenity said.

Bull scowled at the old man. "What the hell you doin' up here, Parker? You're s'posed to be in Columbine, tendin' that privy you call a saloon."

"You'll have to wet your whistle at Mrs. Mondova's," Serenity told the freighter. "Me and Cuno got business. *Manhuntin'* business."

Cuno reproved the old man with a look,

then turned to the freighters. "A pack of owlhoots killed Wade," he explained. "Should be about two days ahead. Call themselves The Committee."

"Ah, shit," Stevens said. "That pack of curly wolves?"

"Seen 'em?"

Stevens jerked a gloved thumb over his shoulder. "Hell, one of 'em is laid up at Heaven's Bane. Seen him last night. Some girl they had with 'em ran a pigsticker through his jaws."

Lyle laughed and scratched his flabby, bare bicep, red and swollen from an insect bite. "Pinned his head to a wardrobe! Ugly damn mess. Still got blood on the floor, and the poor bastard's upstairs howlin' like a trapped timber wolf."

Cuno glanced at Kong. The Chinaman stared at the two freighters, wide-eyed, veins bulging in his forehead.

Cuno looked at Bull. "The others?"

"Headed up the trail. We met 'em on the trail yesterday. Still had the girl with 'em. They hoorawed our mules out of sheer orneriness."

"Damn near ran us off the road," said Lyle. "If we hadn't already off-loaded our freight, we'd be toothpicks at the bottom of Pilgrim's Gulch."

"Least your pecker wouldn't be pussin' up," Bull told him. "Shit, I can smell it on you!"

"Have a good one, boys." Cuno flicked the reins across the mules' backs. As the wagon rolled forward, Cuno favored Kong with another glance.

The Chinaman stared ahead, his brows like a black anvil hooding his eyes. "I knew she would fight."

"At least she's still alive, Kong," Serenity said gently.

"Yesterday," Kong grunted. "What of today?"

Li Mei winced when the horse she rode double with the outlaw leader, Cannady, faltered suddenly as the man turned in his saddle to shout over the girl's head. "Rock farmers' camp — fifty yards an' closin'!"

The man whooped with glee.

Li Mei winced again, this time at the man's loud, grating voice in her ears. The Chinese girl, who knew more English than her parents' native tongue, leaned out from the horse slightly to see around the man's broad, sweaty back. Ahead, tents and plankboard shacks appeared along a narrow, sun-dappled stream.

Men stood knee-deep in the stream, working over long, wooden boxes mounted on legs. Some swirled sand and water in tin pans, staring into the pans intently, the brims of their floppy hats pushed off their foreheads. Several women worked along with the men, working in the water or slinging picks or shovels along the rocky banks. Some carried babies in makeshift packs or watched over others playing in the sand along the shoreline.

Behind Li Mei, other men whooped. She heard the big black man, whose name she'd learned was Brown, laugh his raucous guffaw. It gave her gooseflesh and pricked the hair on the back of her neck.

Cannady spurred the horse into a gallop, and Li Mei closed her tied hands about his waist, pressed her face against his back with an expression of deep distaste, hating the fetor of the man's shirt, the slick, wet feel of his sweat against her cheek. She had no choice but to cling to the man, however. With her hands tied about his waist, if she slipped off the horse's back, she'd merely dangle off a hip. Cannady would probably let her drag.

"Fuckin' rock pickers!" the outlaw leader shouted as the horse galloped into the encampment, setting dogs barking and babies crying.

The other outlaws spread out on both sides of Cannady and Li Mei, several triggering pistols. Brown kicked over a tent while another man leaned out from his horse to upend a wrought-iron spit upon which several birds roasted. One of the prospectors — tall, bearded, wearing a hat and a begrimed, white undershirt — ran out from behind a canvas-and-wood cabin, several split logs in his arms.

"Hey, what the hell you think you're doin'?" he shouted, red-faced with fury.

Cannady slowed his horse. He grabbed a coiled rope off his saddle horn, raised a loop above his head, and swung it out to the right. It settled over the bearded miner's head. Li Mei's eyes widened in astonishment as Cannady jerked the rope taut around the prospector's shoulders, laughing.

As the horse plunged on past the prospector, the man screamed and dropped the wood as the taut rope jerked him off his feet so quickly he seemed to dive forward, as if into a stream — but with his arms clamped to his sides.

He looked up as the rope dragged him along the ground, losing his hat, gritting his teeth, and cursing. He grabbed the rope in both hands, apparently trying to steer himself around obstacles while trying to squirm out from under the taut loop.

As Cannady made for the other end of the settlement, the man plowed through a small cook fire, showering sparks and stretching his lips back from his teeth as he screamed. His clothes and hair smoked for a time as he smashed through sage shrubs and haycocks, and bounced over hummocks and tree stumps. He skidded across a rocky freshet with a splash, mud basting his face.

Li Mei stared so intently at the poor prospector, her eyes wide with horror, that she was only vaguely aware of the destruction and terror the other riders wreaked to both sides of her and Cannady — shooting out windows, kicking over tents and small wagons, and sending the prospector families running for their lives. Ahead of her on the saddle, Cannady loosed several celebratory whoops, guffawing and throwing his head back on his shoulders, flicking occasional looks behind to appraise his work with the fishtailing prospector.

"No!" Li Mei heard herself plead. "Stop!"

As the man plowed through the bare yard of a small cabin, two dogs chasing him and barking and nipping at his trouser cuffs, the rope slid up over his shoulders and head, releasing him. Li Mei felt relief as the man rolled to a dusty stop at the edge of the cabin yard.

She closed her eyes as Cannady continued straight on past the village. Li Mei could hear the thunder of the others galloping behind her, but she didn't open her eyes to see. She didn't open her eyes again until, a few minutes later, the horse's stride slowed.

She peered around Cannady. Ahead and right of the wagon trail they'd been following, a small cabin sat in a meadow between the creek and the pine forest carpeting a high mountain slope. The cabin was one of the biggest Li Mei had seen lately — two stories with a lean-to addition, constructed of peeled, upright pine poles. The windows were filled with real, albeit grubby-looking, glass.

Several corrals and pens stood to the right, a barn to the left.

At the moment, a girl with sandy-blond hair was throwing slop to red chickens in a small, fenced pen. To Li Mei's left, a tall, stoop-shouldered man wearing a coonskin cap was hauling two wooden water buckets, each attached to an end of the pole draped across his shoulders, up from the creek. Under the water's weight, the tall man walked as though trudging through mud. He looked up from the furry brim of his cap, glowering at the riders gathering in his yard under a thick dust cloud.

Cannady regarded the man in the fur cap with passing interest. His gaze settled on the sandy-haired young woman who wore a homespun shirt and denim trousers, her hair gathered in a ponytail. Barefoot, one hand shading her eyes, she stood regarding the group from inside the pen, with an expression much like that of the tall man's.

The cabin door opened and two more girls stepped out. One — short, dark, and round-faced — appeared around Li Mei's age, thirteen. The other, taller and with hair the same color as the girl in the chicken pen, looked to be around seventeen or eighteen.

All three were pretty. The two oldest girls filled out their dresses.

Li Mei gave a silent sob, castigating herself for the relief she felt. Tonight, these girls would no doubt take some of the attention away from her.

13

"What can I do fer you gents?"

It was the tall, bearded man in the coonskin cap. He'd apparently figured out who the gang's leader was, and while Cannady was raking his eyes across the three comely young ladies, the man had stopped near Cannady's horse. The man slid his brown eyes between the group's leader and Li Mei, the bridge of his nose wrinkled with apprehension and curiosity.

Cannady spat a wad of dust and saliva onto a rock near one of the man's hobnailed boots, and wiped his mouth with the back of his gloved hand. "Well, now, it ain't what you can do for us, amigo. It's what *we* can do for *you.*"

The wooden pole sagging across his shoulders, the bearded man raked his eyes across the gang nearly filling the cabin's small yard, horses blowing and swishing their tails, a couple drawing water from a stock trough near the barn. His face was long and weathered, the skin drawn tight to the bones, with a purple mole on the nub of his right cheek. His furry chin pointed like an angry finger at Cannady.

"How's that?"

"We come bearing gifts!"

Cannady glanced at Young Knife and El Lobo, both of whom sat their horses several yards off the right hip of Cannady's mount. Small, bloodstained mountain goats were draped over the rumps of both horses, the horned heads hanging slack down one side, rear legs sagging down the other.

The open eyes of both goats appeared to be taking in the scene with wan disinterest.

"My *compadres* there," Cannady said, canting his head toward Young Knife and El Lobo, "shot 'em a couple mountain goats a few miles back. We were thinkin' about stoppin' early today and havin' us a nice, big bonfire and a mountain goat supper. How'd it be if you and your girls do the cookin' and servin' in exchange for the succulent meat of two prime young goats fattened off Rocky Mountain wild grass and willow leaves?"

Cannady grinned down at the man expectantly, one hand holding his reins, the other resting on his thigh.

The man said nothing, only studied the gang thoroughly, flicking his wary glance back to Cannady and the Chinese girl riding, hang-headed and bruised, behind him. To Cannady's left, the creek gurgled between its sandy banks. To his right, the chickens clucked. One of the two girls at the house's open front door muttered something to the other one, too softly for Cannady to hear.

Finally, Ned Crockett gigged his horse up to Cannady's left. The oldest of the gang members slid his long-barreled .44 from his tied-down holster and held it negligently across his saddle horn, aimed in the general direction of the bearded gent. He canted his head at the man, spreading a toothy grin.

"The only acceptable answer here, sir, is yes."

The bearded man scowled.

Cannady threw up his right hand and twisted around in his saddle to regard the others. "It's a deal, boys. The man says *yes*. We provide the food, they serve!"

While the others whooped victoriously and gigged their tired mounts toward the barn, Cannady cast his glance toward the chicken coop. The full-figured, sandy-blond girl stood just outside the pen's door, her empty slop pail in one hand. Her other hand was fisted on her hip. She cocked one foot, canted her head to the side, and slitted one eye at him.

Cannady chuckled and gigged his horse up the slight hill, turned the horse sideways to the girl, and stopped. He closed the lid over his bad eye and grinned down at her.

"Hidy, there. Name's Cannady."

The girl's pretty, heart-shaped face was implacable. "You're outlaws, ain't you?"

"Yes, ma'am. *Dangerous* ones too."

The girl flushed slightly. Her chest heaved, full breasts pushing at the rough wool shirt. She dropped her eyes to the six-shooter thonged on his right thigh. "You kill many people with that?"

Cannady slipped the gun from its holster, raised it barrel-up, and spun the cylinder. "Oh, only about a hundred."

"A hundred? I don't believe you!"

"Well, maybe only eighty-five or ninety. I lost track around fifty." Cannady chuckled, dropped the pistol back in its holster, and leaned toward the girl, resting his forearm on his thigh. "What's your name?"

"Aubrey."

"Aubrey, the slanty-eye behind me is Li Mei. She's a captive. A war trophy, you might call her. I'm taking her to a whore-house in Sundance 'cause the man who

170

owns the place, a cousin of mine, likes slanty-eyed whores. I owe him a whore 'cause I killed one of his. Anyways, I'm tryin' to keep Li Mei in as good a shape as possible, so I sure would appreciate it if, when I've done tied her to that little willow tree yonder, you'd bring her a cup of water." He grinned. "Would you do that for ole Cannady?"

Aubrey glanced at Li Mei, then slid her combatant gaze back to the outlaw leader. "Who're you to give me orders?"

"The man who done killed upward of a hundred people, half of those women who sassed me." Cannady winked. "That's who. Now, you do as you're told, girl, and maybe I'll give you a couple sips of whiskey around the fire tonight. How'd that be?"

The girl stared at him, the flush in her cheeks growing slightly. Her eyes flicked to his pistol, then back to his face. Sweat glistened faintly on her forehead.

Cannady pinched his hat brim. "See you later, Miss Aubrey." He reined his horse around and gigged it toward the barn.

When Cannady and the other men had unsaddled their horses in the barn, then turned them into the corral, Cannady tied Li Mei to the willow between the yard and the creek. He pinched the girl's cheek and gave her a brusque kiss on the lips, telling her not to fret and that she should thank him, Cannady, for not killing her after what she'd done to Paxton, or turning her over to his men.

"They'd make an awful mess of your delicate face," he said, caressing her cheek with the knuckles of his right hand, her fearful, bruised eyes canted down. "What a surprise you'll be to ole Len Owen. I don't understand it myself, but he likes you slanty-eyes. Apparently, the miners in Sundance do too."

He shrugged, spat, picked up his saddlebags and bedroll, and headed toward the fire pit in the middle of the yard, where the other men were throwing down their gear — tired and dusty and happy to be stopping early for the night.

Li Mei watched him throw his saddle down beside that of the man called Crockett, kicking Crockett jokingly and telling him he'd better not snore as loud as last night or Cannady would fix his throat with a Green River knife. Crockett responded with something Li Mei couldn't hear because the other men were gathering around them, laughing and joking and punching each other lightly, a couple pretending to be

172

fighting over which one was going to get which of the prospector's three daughters later.

Li Mei didn't care that she couldn't hear Cannady. She'd only been listening to distract herself from her own misery — her bruised face and her wrists into which the ropes had cut deeply.

She'd probably never see her father again.

Her mother was dead, buried back in New Mexico after dying from smallpox, and now her father would be alone, as Li Mei would be alone, earning her keep by spreading her legs for filthy miners in a whorehouse in a town she hadn't known even existed until two days ago.

She'd heard stories of such women.

Women who often died from disease or lived beyond their attractiveness and were thrown like refuse into the streets.

Poor Papa.

As she thought of him, the tears came, Li Mei's lower lip quivering. She leaned as far forward as the ropes tying her wrists behind the tree would allow. Then she merely sobbed, her long, black hair hanging like two raven wings on either side of her face.

Lost in her own misery, she didn't know how much time had passed before soft footsteps rose above the din of the talking, laughing renegades. A shadow moved before her, and she snapped her head back, terrified that one of them was going to . . .

"Easy," said a girl's voice coldly.

Li Mei opened her eyes.

Before her crouched the blond girl Cannady had talked to. She squatted before Li Mei, holding a battered tin cup of water. The girl had put on a dress and combed her hair, drawing it back in a French braid, and she'd scrubbed the dirt from her face. Li Mei glanced at the hand holding the cup six inches before Li Mei's chin. Aubrey had even dug some of the dirt out from beneath her fingernails.

"Drink it," Aubrey said, her voice sharp with impatience. "He wants you to drink, so drink. I got work to do."

Li Mei peered over Aubrey's left shoulder. The girl's sisters, who were still dressed as they had been when the gang had ridden into the cabin yard, were digging old ashes from the fire pit. The men lounged around, leaning against their saddles and passing bottles, leering at the girls and offering lewd comments. Shoveling ashes into a wheelbarrow, the girls ignored them.

Li Mei shuttled her glance back to the cup, tipped her head toward it. The girl lifted the cup slightly, and Li Mei drank half the water, surprised by her thirst, feeling somewhat refreshed by the cold creek water.

"All right, you had your drink, ya damn heathen." Aubrey stood, shaking out the last few drops from the cup. "Papa said your kind worships the devil — that true?"

Li Mei stared up at her, too distraught to respond. It wasn't as if she hadn't heard such questions before. Papa had said that in the land where he and Li Mei's mother had come from, before Li Mei was born, they weren't bothered by such questions, and the girl often wondered what that would be like.

Holding the cup down against her thigh, Aubrey glanced back toward the men sitting around the fire pit. "You lay with him — Cannady?"

Li Mei recoiled slightly, nauseated, and shook her head quickly.

"How come? He might go easier on ya if ya pleasure him right."

When Li Mei didn't respond, Aubrey said, "Is it the eye?" She chuckled. "Gotta admit, he ain't real pleasant to look at, but I'd lay with him. Hell, to get outta here I'd lay with the devil himself." Aubrey stared down at Li Mei coldly, then chuffed and turned away. "Nice chattin' with ya."

As Aubrey headed back through the yard,

weaving around the men, Cannady spotted her and jerked down the bottle he'd been drinking from. "Hey, there's my girl!"

He reached out and gave Aubrey's dress a tug. Aubrey leapt away, laughing, and jogged off to the cabin, her hair falling from the French braid and spilling about her shoulders. Cannady and several other men whooped behind her.

A large bonfire was built, the goats roasted on a high, iron spider which the prospector, Mason Llewellyn, had forged from wrought iron and wagon wheel scraps. He and the girls served coffee and beans to go with the meat the men grabbed from the spit and ate with their fingers, stumbling around drunk, howling and joking and expostulating the ways in which they'd spend the money they intended to rob from the bank at Sundance.

One of the men played rousing numbers on his fiddle in spite of one broken string, singing along when he could remember the words.

Seen from afar, the shindig before the cabin would have looked like some other-worldly barbaric frenzy, possibly one of unmentionable witchery or human sacrifice. All that was needed were buxom barbarian wenches strolling the crowd in bare feet, pouring ale from pewter pitchers, to complete the picture.

All the gang had, however, were the "yellow devil wench," whom Cannady had deemed untouchable, and the prospector's three daughters, only one of whom seemed, when her father wasn't casting admonishing looks her way, to enjoy the festivity.

The blond Aubrey strolled about the crowd with a bean kettle or coffeepot, taking furtive sips from Cannady's bottle or puffs off his cigarette, as she refilled the men's cups and tin plates. It wasn't long before she was stumbling over gear and tack, giggling and laughing and no longer swatting the men's brazen hands away from her breasts and ass, letting her dress hang open halfway down her chest to reveal a good portion of her corset-lifting cleavage.

It was only nine o'clock, but good dark, when the prospector shuttled his other two daughters into the cabin, to the whining protests of several hard cases.

When both daughters had disappeared inside, Llewellyn turned from the cabin door, one hand on the knob, gazing across the crowd milling in the shadows shunted this way and that by the fire.

"Aubrey?"

The girl didn't hear him. A couple of horses had gotten out of the corral because someone hadn't latched the gate, and Brown and Crocodile Burdette were drunkenly hazing them back in, making a ruckus, the horses stomping around and nickering loudly. Meanwhile, Aubrey was sitting beside Cannady, knees drawn up to her breasts, holding a near-empty bottle by the neck.

Cannady, resting one elbow on his saddle, caressed the girl's face with a hay stem.

"You mean," Aubrey said, slurring her words, her eyes heavy, "you boys're sorta like the James and Younger gangs in the illustrated newspaper . . . ?"

"Ha!" Cannady ran the end of the hay stalk between the girl's full lips. "They're kinda sorta like *us!* But not quite. They'd like to be just *half* as ornery and mean as —"

"Aubrey, goddamn your hide, girl!" It was the tall prospector, stumbling through the reclining men toward Cannady and Aubrey. He clutched a rusty, long-barreled shotgun in both hands across his chest. "What the hell you think you're doin' out here? Didn't you hear me callin' you?"

Cannady snapped his head at him, the tattoo under his milky eye turning bright green against the crimson planes of his savage face. "Light a shuck, old man. Can't you see I'm talkin' to your daughter?"

"Filth!" Llewellyn shouted. "Pure filth. An' I won't put up with you carryin' on with my whore of a daughter on my own property!"

"I told you to light a shuck, you old bastard," Cannady raked out through gritted teeth. His expression softened, his lips curling a mirthless grin. "Me and your daughter are discussin' our future together."

"Future, hell!" The old man stepped back and lowered the shotgun. "I'm warnin' you, Cannady!"

"I ain't gonna warn *you!*" Cannady had slid his .45 from its holster. He extended the pistol casually in his right hand, thumbing the hammer back and leveling the barrel at the prospector's gut.

Aubrey cast a horrified glance at Cannady. "Wait! No!"

The Remington leapt in Cannady's hand, the resolute crack echoing flatly. Llewellyn's shirt puffed and smoked. The man, who had begun cocking the single-bore's hammer, stumbled back as if punched. His eyes snapped wide, and the shotgun sagged in his hands.

"Papa!" Aubrey screamed, dropping the

whiskey bottle and lurching forward.

Cannady grabbed the girl by the back of her dress, pulled her against him. "Get down here and spread your legs, bitch!"

She flailed her hands toward her father as Cannady grabbed her around the waist. "Let me go!"

Several of the men chuckled. One of the horses, whose head stall was held by Brown, gave a frightened whinny.

"Jesus, Cannady!" mockingly exclaimed Ned Crockett. "That ain't no way to treat our host!"

As Llewellyn dropped the shotgun and fell to his knees, the cabin door creaked open. The head of the oldest girl poked out. Her voice was tentative. "Papa?"

Llewellyn fell face-forward in the dirt.

"Papa!" screamed the prospector's oldest, bolting out of the cabin and running toward her father. The other girl came out as well, following her sister with halting footsteps, a terrified light in her young eyes.

While Cannady wrestled Aubrey down to his blanket roll, tearing at her dress, El Lobo tripped the oldest daughter. She sprawled in the dust beside her father. The Indian, Young Knife, gave a whoop and threw himself atop the screaming girl.

Several of the other men began stalking

toward the cabin, ten yards in front of which the youngest girl had stopped to regard them owl-eyed. Cannady slapped Aubrey hard across her face and ripped her corset open. As the girl sagged back across his saddle, his eyes glistened down at the two firm, pale mounds of nipple-tipped flesh jutting up at him.

He gave another pull at the dress, the wash-worn fabric ripping away from her bare legs.

Cannady howled. Kneeling between the girl's spread legs, he began unbuckling his cartridge belt. Someone grabbed his shirt from behind, gave it a couple of irritating tugs.

"Cannady, look!"

He glanced at Germany Sale standing behind him. The big, red-bearded man was staring back along the trail, where a dozen or so blazing torches jounced toward the cabin yard, growing larger and larger in the darkness.

Cannady's hands froze on his belt buckle as he stared at the crowd moving toward him.

"Well, I'll be damned," Cannady said, wistful. "Looks like we got comp'ny."

14

Hearing the single gunshot from the direction of Llewellyn's cabin, the nine torch-bearing prospectors from the plundered camp stopped on the trail as a group.

They stared toward the bonfire stabbing its six-foot flames at the stars — an orange, ragged glow in the pitch-black night.

The creek gushed through the rocks on their left — a steady, liquid whoosh punctuated by the hollow chugs of the riffle over Dan's Trough on the far side of the cut. Their wind-battered torches roared like dragons' breath, rife with the stench of tar and coal oil.

Behind the men, their own and the other prospector families had finally stopped reassembling their camp to build a few small supper fires. They'd have to resume the cleanup the next day — thanks to the renegades who'd thrashed tents and board shacks and strewn the families' meager belongings out of sheer wickedness.

One man was dead. Two more wounded.

As if life wasn't hard enough.

"Did ye hear that?" said Chet Hurley, turning toward his tent mate, Junior Duffy. They'd been tent mates before their tent had been knocked down and torn to shreds, that is. "Pistol shot."

"Think I'm deaf?" grunted Duffy.

The group stood frozen, holding their old-model rifles in their sweat-slick hands. Only one man — Dwight Pearson — had a new Winchester repeater. Johnny Reinhold had an old, brass-framed Confederate pistol, heavy as a clothes iron, which he backed up with a rock pick in his other hand, the long ash handle wound with rawhide.

Finally, Bill Anderson, standing at the group's rear, chuffed impatiently. Carrying his double-bore Greener in his right hand, his torch in the other, he pushed his way to the front of the group. In spite of his injured leg, sprained neck, two black eyes, and a variety of cuts and bruises over his entire body — all incurred when the gang leader had dragged him behind his horse — Anderson bulled between Hurley and Duffy and limped ahead along the trail, striding toward Llewellyn's cabin.

"What'd you expect 'em to be carryin',

you damn fairies — feather dusters?"

"Come on," said Finn McGraw, the stocky man standing behind Hurley. The gang had pulled his tent down on top of him while he'd been napping, and a bloody bandage covered his left ear, which had nearly been sliced off by his chimney pipe. "Those sons o' bitches can't get by with what they did to our camp. And them throwin' down in Llewellyn's yard, rubbin' our noses in it!"

"I never did care for Llewellyn," said Magpie Henderson, the newest man in the group, who was also married to the prettiest girl in the camp. "He's got airs, preferrin' to live alone and all . . ."

"It ain't about Llewellyn or his daughters," said Reinhold, bulling ahead of the group and following in Anderson's footsteps. "They shot my brother!"

As Reinhold's shadow moved off toward Anderson, whose vague, limping silhouette flickered against the distant fire in Llewellyn's yard, the other group members glanced at each other, their expressions hovering somewhere between rage and terror.

They swallowed, wiped sweat from their faces, renewed their grips on their weapons and their torches, and resumed their trek up the trail toward the cabin.

Anderson was the first one in the yard.

He stopped at the edge of the firelight, looking around at the saddles, bags, and other gear cast willy-nilly around the fire.

The fire itself had burned down to half the size it had been when Anderson and the others had left their own camp. Around it, the hard-packed yard was deserted. The only sounds were the fire, the chickens clucking around their pen, and the horses blowing and stomping inside the corral on the other side of the barn.

Anderson tossed his torch into the fire, gripped his shotgun in both hands across his chest, and glowered into the shunting shadows. Scuff marks and two parallel furrows, like those of a dragged body, curved around the cabin's left wall.

Footsteps rose behind him as the others gathered to either side, breathing hard, their tension almost palpable.

"Where are they?" Reinhold said, a faint trill in his voice.

"Their gear's here," said Hurley, moving forward to kick a saddlebag while casting his gaze about the yard.

"It's a trap." Finn McGraw held his rifle straight out from his belly, sliding the barrel this way and that as he sidestepped around the fire. "Someone check the cabin. We'll cover you."

"I'll do it," grunted Anderson, limping around the fire toward the cabin's front door.

The other men strode slowly behind him, stepping wide of the fire. They'd all tossed their torches into the flames and, all except for Johnny Reinhold, held their weapons in two hands. Reinhold held his old Spiller & Burr revolver in his right hand, the pick straight up in his left.

Anderson was fifteen feet from the door when the latch clicked. The door opened a foot, closed again with a resounding slam. A half second later, it opened two feet and a naked girl bolted out, running and screaming, *"Noooo!"*

Anderson hunched his shoulders and leveled his shotgun, freezing as the girl ran toward him, her red face crumpled with horror. "Help me!"

A man's voice raked through the gap in the cabin door. "God*damnit!*"

Anderson pressed his index finger against his two-bore's left trigger, but stopped short of squeezing. If he'd fired the barn blaster, he'd surely have cut the blonde — Llewellyn's middle girl — in two. She ran around behind him, sobbing, "They shot Poppa and they're gonna kill us too!"

Anderson glowered with annoyance as the

186

girl gripped his shirt, as if trying to position him between her and the hard cases.

"Stop that now, damnit, gir— !"

He clipped the sentence as a man stepped out of the cabin holding a long-barreled revolver in one hand. He held the other hand to his mouth, his lips closed over the knuckle of that index finger.

He was a broad-shouldered hombre with a weathered Stetson shading one good eye, the right one appearing strangely pale. A small red-and-green tattoo of some sort had been scratched into his right cheek, just above his thin, black beard.

"Bitch bit me!" he protested.

The other prospectors froze behind Anderson, who could hear their frightened grunts and breathless exclamations to his right and left flanks.

The tattooed gent looked over Anderson's right shoulder, his face pinched with anger as he shook his pistol straight out at the end of his arm. "You'll pay for that, you fucking *whore!*"

The girl clutched Anderson's shirt, pinching some skin along with it, cowering, shifting her weight from one bare foot to the other. "Please don't let him kill me!"

Another man had stepped out beside the first — slightly shorter and dressed in a black frock and whipcord trousers. A tan duster hung to his calves, both sides pulled back from a fancy brace of silver-plated pistols.

"What the hell happened, Cannady?"

"Shut up, Case!" Cannady barked, glaring at the girl hidden behind Anderson. "Bitch bit me and lit out. It was so dark, I couldn't see a thing."

Ignoring Cannady, the man called Case raised up on his boot toes and, sweeping his deep-set eyes across the small crowd gathered before him, grinned. He'd left both pistols in their holsters and appeared in no hurry to remove them.

Somehow, Anderson took vague comfort in that . . . in spite of the girl cowering behind him, pinching his bruised back. The shock of the two renegades' abrupt appearance had caused him to lower his shotgun's barrel, and for some reason the gun suddenly weighed a ton.

"Hidy, gents!" Case said in greeting. "How y'all doin' this evenin'?" In the dark cabin behind him, another girl sobbed. He turned sharply. "You shut up in there! Don't wanna have to tell you again."

The sobbing stopped abruptly, as if a hand had been clapped across the girl's open mouth.

Annoyed by the blonde behind him using him as a shield, Anderson turned around, grabbed her bare arm, and gave her a shove. "Get away!"

The girl fell in the dirt, crying, her full breasts jiggling.

Anderson swung back, raising the shotgun slightly, narrowing his eyes at the two men on the cabin's porch. "Where's the rest of you sons o' bitches?"

He'd remembered the face of the man who'd dragged him — the tattooed face of the man standing left of the handsome, black-clad hard case. Anderson's bowels burned with fury.

He'd blow his kneecaps off, kill him slow!

"They're just over there," said Cannady, canting his head toward Anderson's left.

"Shee-it!" Anderson recognized the voice of Lloyd Talbot, heard the scuffs as the other prospectors jerked to the right.

On the east side of the cabin, at the edge of the yard, just under a dozen hard cases stood facing Anderson and the other prospectors. Their eyes glistened coldy in the fire's dying light. None of the renegades held a pistol or a rifle, but their hands hung down over their holsters, like coiled snakes ready to strike.

The only one smiling was the black man,

his black hat tipped over his eyes, pink lips curled back from two rows of chipped, marble teeth. He made no sound, but his heavy shoulders jerked with silent laughter.

"Sure enough," said Cannady with glee, as if introducing old friends whom the prospectors hadn't seen in a while. "There's old Ned and Whinnie and Lobo, and the big ole cowpoke Crocodile Burdette. And then there's grinnin' Brown and Germany Sale, and . . . ah, hell . . . those names don't mean nothin' to you, do they?"

"Nah," said the handsome gent standing beside Cannady. "They's just the names o' the men's gonna kill you — that's all."

Anderson swallowed, squeezed his shotgun so tight he felt as though blood were about to surge out from under his fingernails. Behind him, the others shuffled their feet and swallowed loudly. Anderson thought he could hear their hearts pounding, but then, he couldn't hear much of anything above the thunder of his own.

"You . . . you had no right to do what ye done!" he heard himself say, as if his own voice were speaking of its own accord from the bottom of a deep well.

"Yes, we did," said Cannady with a reasonable smile.

"Sure we did," said the handsome gent

beside him.

Both replies took Anderson aback. He glanced behind, was relieved to see the others still back there, shuttling glances between the two groups of renegades.

Anderson turned back to Cannady, cocked his head to one side. "How's that?"

The handsome gent tipped his chin up, chuckling. " 'Cause we *could!*"

Cannady looked pleasantly surprised at the handsome man's response. "Yeah." He laughed. "Yeah, that's it. We had every right to do what we done . . . 'cause we *felt* like it!"

Anderson stared at him, the prospector's blood boiling. He gritted his teeth so hard he could hear his molars crack.

"Bastards!" He raised the shotgun and fired, the boom echoing above the pounding of his own heart.

He watched in disbelief as the pellets blew a tub-sized hole in the cabin door, where the two renegades had been standing before. Seeing him raise the shotgun, they'd leapt to either side. The handsome man clawed iron so fast that his gloved hand was a blur above his black, silver-trimmed holster.

Anderson saw flames blossom before the handsome gent's right hip. The prospector felt merely a heavy, wet sensation in his chest as he thumbed back the shotgun's second hammer. But when he began aiming the two-bore toward the cabin, he realized he was in trouble.

The gun suddenly weighed even more than before.

It sagged in his arms as, hearing gun blasts and seeing smoke rising before him left and right, he glanced down. Blood frothed like a fountain from his chest, gushing down his denim shirt and over his belly to his crotch.

Muffled screams rose behind Anderson as he dropped the shotgun and, legs turning to water, dropped to his knees.

He sagged onto his hip and elbow, turned his head slowly to his right. On her knees, the naked blonde had opened her mouth and eyes wide. While Anderson could hear little but the blasts of gunfire, he knew she was screaming, holding her hands out before her as if to shield herself from the bullets.

It didn't do any good. She'd already taken one through her left breast, an inch above the nipple.

And now, as Anderson watched, his vision dimming as his own life ebbed, several more bullets plunked into her chest and face, spraying blood and throwing her straight back away from Anderson, her hair, arms, and legs windmilling before she hit the ground on her back.

Beyond her, most of Anderson's compatriots were down, rolling, awash in blood, and screaming.

Only Finn McGraw stood, arms and legs bloody, firing his old Zuave carbine toward the right. Aiming the old Confederate rifle like the good Reb sharpshooter he'd been.

Anderson didn't know what happened after that. His head sagged back against the ground. His eyes rolled into his head. His torn heart stopped.

His arms and legs shook for a time before McGraw fell over them in a bloody heap.

Then it was McGraw whose death spasms wracked his stocky frame for a time, before both prospectors lay limp in death, one atop the other.

15

"Afternoon, ladies," Cuno Massey said, pinching his hat brim and squinting against the wagon dust catching up to him.

He, Serenity Parker, and the Chinaman, Kong, had just pulled up to the big, sprawling, unpainted barracks that was the Heaven's Bane Whorehouse, Saloon, and Gambling Parlor. Spread out upon the raised front stoop before them, a dozen or so girls lounged about the wicker chairs, bar stools, and porch rail, taking the cool, clear afternoon air. One of them played with a frisky, red retriever pup in her lap, the dog trying to chew her earrings.

Blackbirds were lined up on one of the roof's several peaks, taking in the strangers with black-eyed interest, occasionally giving an inquiring caw.

"Hidy," said a small blonde sitting the railing in only her pantaloons and low-cut chemise, one arm on a rail post as she regarded the three newcomers over her left shoulder. "You boys stoppin' early for the day?"

Serenity Parker wheezed a chuckle and ran a gloved hand across his sunburned nose. "She's purty as a speckled pup!"

The oldster meant the compliment only for Cuno's ears, but the blonde had heard him. She turned her head to him, her smile growing. "Well, thank you, sir. You look like a man needin' a special dance — the mattress kind." She winked.

Serenity wheezed another, louder laugh, coloring up like a desert sunset. "Honey, I'm afraid you'd stop this old heart!"

Several of the girls laughed. On the other side of Serenity, Kong found nothing to laugh at. He stared at the girls with grim purpose, his anxiety showing in his wide, brown eyes, in the veins standing out on his forehead.

"Actually, we ain't here for rompin', ladies. We're lookin' for a Chinese girl." Cuno canted his head toward Kong. "This man's daughter. We were told she rode here with a gang two nights back."

A haggard-looking brunette, leaning against the front wall near the door and smoking a long, black cheroot, blew smoke and chuckled huskily. "I'll say she did. Rode

195

off with 'em too, after running a pigsticker through one man's jaws."

"Right here," said the blonde on the railing, placing a long, pale finger low against her cheek, right about where her jaws hinged. "Pinned to a wardrobe till one of his friends worked him free."

"Gave the girl a good workin' over too," said the brunette, gazing through her windblown hair at Kong. "I'm sorry, mister. There's no tellin' what's happened to her by now."

Breathing sharply, Kong rose in his seat like a slow-blowing volcano. He clenched his fists at his sides. "Where is this sonuv'bitch Li Mei stab? *Where* is?"

All the girls looked at him wistfully. The brunette glanced at Cuno, who sat the wagon, the ribbons in his hands, saying nothing.

The brunette lifted the corners of her thin mouth slightly and shuttled her glance back to Kong. "He's upstairs. Room at the end of the hall. He's been in so much pain, carryin' on so crazy, breakin' things, we had to sedate him with laudanum and whiskey." The corners of her mouth rose still higher. "And a few other things."

Kong turned to Cuno. "We stop here for while." It wasn't a question. The Chinaman pressed his hide-wrapped skinning knife against his belt, as if securing it. He climbed down the other side of the wagon, walked around the mules, and mounted the porch steps. He strode purposefully past the whores, though his moccasins barely made a sound on the unpainted porch planks, and entered the Heaven's Bane by one of its two front doors, leaving the door standing wide open behind him.

The retriever pup had eyed Kong's moccasins devilishly. Now the pup leapt from the whore's lap and, its toenails ticking across the planks, ran floppy-eared into the saloon behind the Chinaman.

"Dan-ny!" called the whore. Droopy-eyed, she gave a disgusted chuff, then took a long sip from her whiskey glass and sat back in her chair, lifting her face to the sun.

The blond whore regarded Cuno and Serenity with smoky eyes. "You boys want a drink or a poke while you're waitin'?"

"Speakin' for myself," Cuno said, wrapping the reins around the brake handle, "I was wonderin' if you gals might have a fast horse in your stable. One I could rent for a few days."

The blonde shrugged and deferred to the tired-looking brunette. "Most of our horses are buggy nags, but every once in a while

197

our humble abode becomes a man's final restin' place . . . if you get my drift. You might be able to find one or two spry orphans out in the corral yonder. We got a hostler out there somewhere — Kimbal Logan — but he's probably fishin' this time of the day. Help yourself. Leave a dollar or two so Kimbal can buy him a new braid o' chaw."

Cuno pinched his hat brim. "Obliged."

He turned to Serenity, staring up at him curiously. "I'm gonna ride ahead, see if I can fetch Kong's daughter. I got a feelin' time's runnin' out for her. You take over the wagon. I'll trail back when I've found her."

"How're you gonna get her back . . . with all them hard cases swarmin' around her?"

Cuno jumped down from the wagon. A cry sounded through the second story's open windows — shrill with anguish and unendurable pain.

A moment later, the retriever pup appeared, bolting out the main doors, slipping on the boards as it turned sharply and leapt into the lap of the whore it had left. The dog whimpered and buried its head in the girl's bosom. The other whores regarded the pup darkly, shuttling their gazes to the yawning front doors as another muffled, anguished cry echoed around inside.

"Oh, Jesus — not again! Help!"

Cuno turned his gaze back to Serenity. "I'll figure that out when I catch up to 'em." He rummaged around in the wagon box for his war bag and bedroll, then grabbed his rifle and headed for the stables flanking the house. "Keep Kong with you."

"You sure you know what you're doin'?" Serenity yelled behind him.

Cuno didn't turn around as he mounted the hill toward the corral and stables. "No."

Cuno chose the only one of the three riding horses in the corral that looked like it still remembered what a saddle was and hadn't been spoiled by oats and long, lazy days following the buggy mares around with its proverbial hat in its hands. The blaze-faced roan was high-stepping and long-legged enough for fast travel, but its broad chest bespoke a good set of lungs as well.

Cuno rigged the horse with a worn but adequate saddle he found in the tack room, then gigged the horse around to the front of the whorehouse, halting beside the wagon. Inside, the wounded hard case was bawling and sobbing like an injured child. At times the voice sounded like that of an enraged, wounded mountain lion.

The bemused whores sat in fascinated

silence, drinking and smoking. The pup was cowering on the floor, its head in its paws, between two slippered feet.

"He still at it?" Cuno asked Serenity.

Tugging anxiously on his beard, the old man turned to Cuno. "What do you think he's *doin'* to him in there?"

"Whatever it is, I wish he'd teach me the trick. It'd come in handy once I run down the leader of those butchering renegades."

As the wails and whines turned to pants and then to a slowly rising squeal, Cuno ground his heels against the roan's flanks. He galloped down the hill and out of the yard, crossing the creek on the wooden bridge, then swerving back onto the main trail toward Sundance.

He soon found the roan was indeed fast as well as a stayer as he and the horse whipped through one canyon and over one pass after another, taking the switchbacks with their heads down, barely slowing for the turns, stopping only for short blows at ridge crests, or for water, or to let an ore wagon or a prospector's supply wagon pass.

The roan was nearly as much horse as Cuno's own paint, Renegade, which he'd left in his own wagon barn in Denver.

He rode hard the first afternoon out from

Heaven's Bane, and camped in a hollow along a creek feeding into the St. Vrain River. Up at false dawn and not bothering with coffee, but only some jerky and dry biscuits, he and the horse galloped over the long, sloping shoulder of Taylor Mountain.

By one o'clock that afternoon, he trotted into a clearing in which a handful of makeshift tents and cabins sat on the north bank of the St. Vrain River.

Cloud shadows scudded. Hammer blows rang out as two stoop-shouldered, gray-haired men erected a shanty wall in a small aspen copse. Several others swirled pans in the river shallows, while a handful of women scrubbed clothes along the shore.

As Cuno rode toward the women, they cast him furtive, fearful glances. A stocky, plain-faced, middle-aged woman with dull red hair falling from her soiled poke bonnet stepped out from the crowd to meet him.

"Just ride on, mister," she said, gritting her teeth and dipping her chin with anger. "We don't want no more trouble!"

Behind her, five other women of various ages seemed to cower as they sidestepped toward the river, holding hands. A few glanced at Cuno warily, then turned to mutter with the others.

Cuno tipped his hat back off his forehead.

"I take it the Clayton Cannady bunch has been through here."

The woman looked at him skeptically, flicked a lock of lusterless red hair from her face. "They sacked our camp, killed a good three quarters of our men, threw 'em in the river like trash. Killed two girls. Took another one for their pleasure." Balling her wet apron in her freckled fists, the woman stared up at Cuno, her eyes flickering around his chest as if looking for something. "You law?"

Cuno shook his head. "I'm on Cannady's trail just the same, though. I aim to kill him and the rest of his horde."

"He run roughshod over your camp too?"

"You could say that. How long since he left here?"

"Yesterday." The woman canted her head upstream. "He left three killers behind. They're waitin' for someone Cannady left farther off down the trail. His kin, or some such. Those three took our weapons and been havin' one heck of a real good time while they wait."

She glanced behind at the other women, several of whom sported bruised faces, including a couple black eyes, then turned back to Cuno. "The menfolk we're left with are either too old or too young or too *wounded* to do anything without a gun."

Cuno looked upstream. He couldn't see much beyond a rocky bend. "Up thataway?"

"They're havin' a swim up beyond that horseshoe," the woman said. "We're supposed to fix 'em a nice meal later . . . when we get done washin' their clothes."

Cuno jerked back on the roan's reins, backing the horse away from the women and the river. "You can stop washing their clothes."

"There's three, and they're poison mean," the woman warned, shading her eyes with her hand. "You best ride on, young fella. Leave 'em to God."

"How 'bout if I leave 'em to the devil?"

Cuno neck-reined the roan and trotted upstream, angling across the horseshoe. A dead, bloated dog lay in the short grass and sage, riddled with bullets and sending up a nose-wrinkling death stench.

When Cuno had ridden seventy yards, he spotted three men splashing in a wide, shallow stretch of river, the stones showing just beneath the surface. The water glittered in the afternoon light, the splashes sending up beaded jewels. Laughter rose above the river's own chuckle over the rocks.

Cuno halted the horse, keeping a low rise between him and the renegades.

Two men in the river. One stood along the shore, his back to Cuno, wearing a soggy pair of wash-worn balbriggans. The standing hard case bent his knees slightly and turned right, his stream of yellow piss arcing high over the water, glistening.

The man farther out in the stream, floating on his back in a shallow pool, shouted, "Quit pissin' in the stream, damn you, Germany!"

"You're making the water unfit fer man or beast!" the other man said with a laugh, lying flat in a sandy patch in the rocky bed, lolling like a dead man, his head thrown back, eyes squeezed shut. Like the other man in the river, he appeared naked.

"Fuck you — I'll piss where I want!" Germany retorted, watching his piss stream die, bending his knees and jutting his hips as if to keep it going.

Several other words were exchanged, but Cuno didn't pay attention. He dismounted from the roan, and looked at the Winchester's worn walnut stock jutting up from the saddle boot.

The rifle could be an awkward instrument at close range. The .45 Colt should be adequate.

Cuno turned and, leading the roan, strode toward the shoreline, where the man who'd been pissing now sat on a boulder, an ankle hiked on a knee, rolling a smoke from a hide makings pouch. A Spencer carbine leaned against the rock near the man's left elbow. He paused while rolling the quirley to brush something off his big left toe.

Cuno stopped fifteen feet behind him, and kicked a rock. The man jerked his head toward him, his long, wet hair plastered against his skull. Water shone in his mustache and beard.

He scowled angrily. "Who the hell're you?"

Cuno stared at him. Suddenly, the .45 was in Cuno's right hand, the hammer cocked. He shot the man on the rock through the bottom of his left foot, shredding the big toe. The man gave a hoarse scream and fell off the rock, grabbing his foot.

"Hey!" cried the man farther out in the river, awkwardly trying to stand.

When Cuno's .45 spoke again, the man stumbled back, clutching his right arm around the bicep.

Cuno turned the barrel slightly right, dropped the barrel a half inch. The man closer to shore was up and running toward the boulder ten feet upstream from Cuno, where several cartridge belts were coiled. Cuno let him get within ten feet of the guns, then snapped a shot through the man's left thigh.

As he grabbed his leg in mid-stride, his feet slipped out from under him, and he fell with a splash and the dull snap of breaking bones.

Grimacing and holding his foot with one hand, the man with the shredded big toe lifted his head and raged, *"What the fuck you think you're doin', you son of a bitch?"*

Cuno shot his left earlobe off.

When the man farther out had gained his feet and was running feebly toward the opposite bank, Cuno stopped him with a .45 slug through the back of his left calf. The man dropped and lolled in a knee-deep pool, gritted teeth flashing white.

The man nearer shore crawled to his hands and knees, blood mixing with the water sluicing off his left thigh. He didn't say anything, only stared with animal fear and fury at Cuno. Splintered bones protruded from his right forearm.

Cuno blew a hole through the man's right elbow. The man screamed and slumped over that hand, smacking his face on a half-submerged rock. He pushed up on his good hand and threw his head back, raging.

Cuno turned.

The stocky, redheaded woman stood

fifteen feet behind him. The other women and girls flanked her. All stared agape into the stream, where the three hard cases lolled, raging and bleeding.

Cuno holstered the .45 and climbed into the saddle. He turned the roan back the way he'd come, and pinched his hat brim at the women. "They're all yours, ladies."

He rode on past the staring women, angling back toward the main trail. He passed several old men and a few youngsters moving toward the stream with curious, fearful frowns on their faces.

When Cuno mounted a knoll fifty yards upstream, pistol shots echoed behind. Laughter rose on the breeze.

He turned in his saddle. The women were lined out along the river, several aiming the hard cases' revolvers toward the water, taking target practice. Cannady's men stumbled around the shallow river — bleeding and clutching their wounded limbs as they dodged the shots and begged for mercy.

Another pistol cracked, and one of the hard cases dropped.

The women laughed and cheered.

Cuno grinned and put the roan into a gallop.

16

It wasn't hard to cut the killers' trail sign. They were among the few horseback riders to have taken the wagon trace in recent days. Judging by the depth and distance of their horses' shod prints — and by the number of times they halted along the trail — the gang was in no hurry.

In fact, the evening of the day he'd left the sacked prospectors' camp, Cuno caught up to them.

They'd bivouacked in a box canyon off the north fork of Destiny Creek, which ran cold and fast off the slopes of Renegade Pass. The mountain loomed in the southwest, its bald slopes mantled with fields of dirty snow. On its northern shoulder sat the booming mining village of Sundance, too low and far away — a good twelve miles — to be seen from this vantage. The water filled the air with the smell of wet grass and rock, water-logged deadfalls, moss, ferns, and mushrooms.

In a chill rain and under a fragrant spruce canopy, his buckskin's collar pulled to his neck, Cuno sat atop the slot canyon's northern rim, a half mile down the canyon from the renegades. Through breaks in the rain and fog settling low over the canyon, he could make out their horses tied to two separate picket lines near the stream on the gorge floor.

Blue camp smoke ribboned skyward through the evergreen canopy, which was so thick that Cuno caught only fleeting glimpses of the gang themselves, milling about the fire — hatted silhouettes in heavy coats or rain slickers.

In spite of the light rain, the air was so quiet he could occasionally hear their voices rising above the stream's roaring descent to Destiny Creek farther below and east.

As he sat scrutinizing the camp and wondering how he was going to get down to the girl — if she was still alive — he saw two men climb the steep walls of slick, black granite on either side of the canyon. Both men carried rifles. The sentries would no doubt spend the night on the ridges overlooking the canyon. Earlier, he'd spotted two men heading down to cover the canyon's narrow mouth.

Damn. They weren't going to make it easy.

He considered waiting until the next day. It was doubtful, though, there'd be an easier place or a better time to spring the girl. In fact, the box canyon's walls might work to his advantage, once he had Li Mei in hand, that is.

He wasn't sure why he was risking his neck. The girl was Kong's worry. But then, in spite of the Chinaman's proficiency with an Indian bow, he seemed so blasted helpless — a black sheep in a foreign land, his daughter taken captive by killers . . .

Cuno might even be able to kill a few of the gang before he got out of the canyon. But then, why push his luck? He'd nab the girl and get her back to her father before running down the gang, preferably one by one or two by two. These were cold-blooded killers, and more than a couple were probably as good with a hogleg as Cuno was.

When he'd considered the best way into the canyon, he hunkered back against the slope and pulled his hat brim over his eyes. Might as well grab some shut-eye. His horse was tethered in another, shallower canyon a half mile north, saddled and ready to split the wind when needed.

He dozed, waking twice. He dreamt of July, and was awakened by the shots that had killed her, his head snapping up so fast that his hat tumbled off his left shoulder.

He looked around, his heart slowing gradually. The darkness pressed close. Through the pine bows, stars made a milky, speckled wash across the heavens. No moon. Just enough light to get him down the canyon wall.

He doffed his hat and grabbed the rope he'd carried in his war bag. It was only twenty feet, but it should take him down the sheerest part of the drop. He'd left his Winchester, too clumsy for climbing, with the horse. He wasn't carrying a spare pistol this trip, so the .45 Colt would have to do.

Nudging the pistol's butt compulsively, he walked slowly up the canyon, keeping away from the lip so the stars wouldn't outline him. A dull orange glow appeared forty yards ahead, around a slight curve in the canyon wall. He stopped and dropped to his haunches. The small, round glow brightened for a second, then, dimming, arced toward the ground.

The picket on this side of the canyon was enjoying a smoke as he strolled along the wall. He seemed to be staying close to the camp.

Cuno moved forward at a crouch, skimming the trees on his left. When he found the route he'd scouted before, he tied the rope around a stout pine. Grabbing the hemp in his gloved hands, he backed slowly down the scaly stone surface of the ridge, weaving between shrubs and blocky chunks of granite and weather-gnarled trees thumbing out from the wall.

When he came to the end of the rope, he leapt to a shelf, landing and bending his knees to absorb the fall. He froze, crouching against the black granite, listening, hoping the thump of his boots hadn't been heard below.

Except for the creek's rush and an occasional owl hoot, silence.

He turned. The stream was a pale silver line twisting through the middle of the gorge. On Cuno's side of it, the fire was a red, flickering smudge below and left, ghostly smoke puffs wisping through the pines. The fire was down, which meant the men were probably asleep. It was a slim chance that the picket on the canyon's other rim could see Cuno against the black granite.

Still, the freighter moved quickly, wanting to be on the wall as briefly as possible.

From the ledge, he climbed down easily, as the grade gentled slightly and there were more pine trunks to break his descent. He appraised each feature of his trail, committing it to memory for when he returned with the girl.

When he reached the canyon floor, he leapt a small rivulet gurgling out from a spring, crossed a deadfall aspen, and stepped on a dry twig.

Crack!

Hissing through his clenched teeth, he stopped and dropped, pressing his chin to the cool, damp ground.

To his ears, the breaking branch had sounded like a rifle shot. Apparently, it had gone unheard in the camp. The killers probably couldn't hear much above the stream's roar. Besides, they were probably relying on their horses and the pickets to warn them of trouble.

Cuno pushed himself to his knees, glanced around with one hand on his pistol butt, then straightened and headed across the canyon toward the creek. The water's thunderous rush should cover any other noises he might make on his way to the camp. There was no breeze to betray his smell.

He pushed quietly through the forest. Gaining the creek, he headed upstream, moving faster now that the water covered the sound of his movements. He spied six of the renegades' horses tethered to his left.

Not sensing him, they remained asleep on their feet, statue-still.

Five minutes later, Cuno lay hunkered down in the brush near the water, between a spruce and a mossy boulder, staring into the clearing where the hard cases lay spread out around the dying fire. Their snores were nearly as loud as the stream to Cuno's right.

It took him another five minutes to pick out the girl — or what he thought was the girl — hunkered on the far side of the fire, under an overarching spruce bow. The small, dark figure, curled under a blanket with no saddle or saddlebag to pillow her head, had to be her.

He retreated ten yards, froze when one of the men called out in his sleep for Margot. The dreamer snickered devilishly. A couple of snores stopped, then started up again. Someone sneezed and smacked his lips.

When he was sure the renegades were asleep once more, Cuno continued to the roiling creek, feeling the refreshing humidity and the spray against his face, then circled around and crabbed toward the girl from the opposite direction.

Under an aspen tree, he paused to stare at the small bundle before him, under a pine bough, trying to figure out which end was her head. Spying a lock of straight, black hair falling from a blanket fold, he crawled even closer. When his face was six inches from her rising and falling shoulder, he rose up on his knees, snaked an arm over her body, and pressed the palm of his hand down hard across her mouth and nose. At the same time, he slid his other arm beneath her slender waist.

The girl was instantly awake, tense in his arms, struggling.

Cuno's own heart pounded as he pulled the blanketed bundle straight back with him, back-crabbing the way he'd come, keeping his left palm taut to the girl's mouth. He gritted his teeth as the girl opened her mouth beneath his palm, expelling muffled screams.

When he was beyond the aspen, he stood and, still clamping one hand across her mouth, lifted her to his waist and dragged her through the brush toward the head of the gorge. He moved swiftly, his own heart racing, lungs burning.

Twenty yards from the camp, he gentled her down to the ground and, keeping his palm over her mouth, knelt before her. She thought he was trying to rape her. Her black eyes blazed panic as she stared up at him, trying to bite him and work her head free of his grasp.

"Easy, damnit!" Cuno whispered. "I'm here to help."

He placed a finger to his lips and eased the pressure on her mouth.

She stopped struggling.

A cautious, befuddled light entered her eyes as she stared up at him, her body slowly relaxing. He removed his hand from her mouth.

"No more screams," Cuno whispered. "I'm gonna get you outta here — back to your father."

He whipped the blanket off her body. She wore denim pants, a torn, gray shirt, and moccasins similar to her father's. Her ankles were tied, her wrists tethered behind her back.

Quickly, keeping his ears pricked for sounds from the camp, Cuno unsheathed his knife and cut the ropes. He sheathed the knife and looked at her. "Can you stand?"

She rolled over, placed her hands on the ground, tried to push herself up. No good. She turned her frightened face to him, her eyes beseeching, a wing of hair across her mouth, as she rubbed her right wrist.

He'd had a feeling that, having been tied for so long, she wouldn't be able to stand, much less run.

"That's all right." Cuno grabbed her arm,

bent his knees, and eased her over his shoulder. "It'll be faster this way anyway."

Moving quickly, he headed back the way he'd come, pausing near the creek to give the camp a quick study. The renegades were still asleep, the creek's roar covering their snores.

So far, so good . . .

He made it back to the canyon wall without incident, carried the girl up the wall, crouching and gritting his teeth against the grade. She grunted and groaned, but otherwise remained silent. He knocked his knee against a rock once and nearly had to set her down, but only gritted his teeth against the pain and kept going.

At the ledge, he eased her down against the rock face.

He kept his voice low as he asked, "Any feeling in your hands and feet yet?"

She flexed her hands, reached down to rub her feet through the moccasins. She lifted her face, the eyes hopeful, even eager. "Some."

Cuno grabbed the end of the rope hanging just above the ledge. Casting a quick glance into the canyon, spying no movement, he pulled the girl to her feet, looped the rope around her waist, and slipknotted it.

"I'm gonna climb to the top and pull you up."

He lunged at a rock a foot above his head, got a grip, and pulled himself up, then reached for another rock, and pulled himself another five feet. He dug his fingers and the toes of his boots into any nook or cranny he could find, relieved to grasp the occasional hidden shelf in the darkness.

As he was hoisting and pulling, his breath came hard, his heart pounding.

Keeping his chin up, he blinking against the sweat stinging his eyes as he climbed. He swiped a hand against his gun butt occasionally, making sure it was there, as he swept the rocks above with his eyes, climbing toward the stars capping the ridge crest.

He climbed for ten minutes, then cast another look toward the ridge. He was closing on it now. Ten feet away.

Adrenaline spurred him onward, and he gripped a gnarled cedar root, planted his boot on a slight lip to his left, then pulled at the root and kicked off his left boot heel. His head was a foot beneath the ridge crest when cigarette smoke filled his nostrils.

A second before he'd identified the smell, his heart leapt.

He edged his eyes above the lip and stared through small rocks and stage tufts.

A man's silhouette sat before him, holding a quirley to his mouth. The quirley glowed, dimly lighting the man's narrow, unshaven face, hawk nose, and the underside of his soiled hat brim. Bandoliers crisscrossed his chest.

The man blew out cigarette smoke as he lifted his rifle in one hand, aimed the barrel at Cuno, and laughed.

"Lookee what I found here!"

The rifle boomed, stabbing flames.

17

Cuno dropped his head beneath the ridge's lip, gritting his teeth as the .44 round carved a furrow across his right temple. Wincing against the instant headache, he pressed his forehead to the stone and clawed his .45 from its holster.

There was a sharp, metallic rasp as the man atop the ridge raked another shell into his rifle's breech.

Digging the fingers of his left hand into the ridge crest above his shoulder, Cuno raised the Colt's barrel above his head and fired three shots.

A grunt and heavy footfall.

Cuno lifted his head to peer into the darkness above the ridge. The man stumbled to Cuno's right. Cursing, he dropped to a knee, clutching his belly with the hand that had been holding the rifle.

Blood dribbling down his temple, Cuno hoisted himself up and over the top, quickly gaining his feet and striding toward the night guard lying in the brush. The man was trying to draw a pistol from a shoulder holster worn over a beaded leather vest. His chest and belly glistened with fresh blood.

Cuno shot him through the forehead, then turned to the ridge, breathing through his mouth as he listened. Below, men were yelling and the horses were stomping around, nickering.

A man yelled, "The Chink's gone!"

A scurry of footfalls beneath the creek's rush, then: "Goddamnit. Someone nabbed her. Saddle the fucking horses!"

Cuno cursed his own blue streak as he sheathed the six-shooter and ran back to the ridge's lip. He grabbed the rope and looked down to where the girl made a vague outline against the rock face. Her face was a brown oval canted toward him.

"I'm haulin' you up!" he yelled loudly enough for only her to hear. "Use your feet if you can."

"I can," came the girlish voice, thin and brittle with fear.

"Now!" Cuno ground his heels into the turf and pulled hand over fist, leaning forward and putting his shoulders into it, his thick neck bulging.

From below sounded the scrapes and

scuffs as the girl rose toward him, kicking off the wall, giving little fearful grunts and groans as she spun and knocked a hip or shoulder against the unforgiving stone.

A man yelled from the other ridge, "Shots came from over there." The voice echoed. Cuno shunted his gaze across the canyon. The other picket was probably standing atop the opposite ridge, pointing in his direction. The man had seen the gun flashes. He could probably even make out Cuno and the girl's figure toiling along the ridge.

"Come on, girl!" Cuno rasped.

Li Mei didn't weigh much — probably not even a hundred pounds — so he had her within an arm's reach in under a minute.

A rifle cracked, an orange flash on the other ridge, directly across from Cuno. The slug shattered against stone well below the girl.

Holding the rope taut in one hand, Cuno reached down with the other and grabbed her arm. The picket on the opposite ridge fired again, the slug cracking off a rock a good ten yards below and left. Cuno pulled the girl straight up and set her down beside him.

She tripped over her own feet and fell. She was a gamer, though, and quickly pulled herself to her feet. She'd heard the men and the horses scrambling around in the canyon, as Cuno had. Panting, she shook her hair from her eyes and looked up at Cuno expectantly.

In the canyon below, the men yelled more shrilly, arguing over who'd been watching the girl, no doubt. There were indistinct thumps and rustles as the killers scrambled to saddle their horses.

Two rifles barked almost at once, the slugs plunking into the brush and rocks at Cuno's and the girl's feet.

A couple of hard cases, keying on the pickets' shots, were shooting from directly below.

Cuno grabbed the girl's arm and pulled her away from the ridge lip, then crouched to regard her gravely. "I've got a horse about two hundred yards that way. Think you can make it?"

"I can make it!"

Several more shots sounded, the slugs spanging off the ridge's brushy, rocky lip.

Automatically, Cuno grabbed his rope from the tree and quickly coiled it over his arm. He took the girl's hand and began running away from the canyon. "Let's go!"

She limped along boldly for a while, but after thirty yards she slowed, her knees bending. She sobbed. "My feet are still numb!"

"I've got you!" Cuno turned, stooped, threw her over his shoulder, and resumed running, the girl flopping on his arm and down his back as he leapt sage shrubs and rabbitbrush.

The girl didn't weigh much, but she'd begun to feel twice her weight by the time he'd gained the opposite ridge crest and started his descent. Halfway down, he stopped, set her down against a boulder, and dropped to one knee. He canted his head, listening.

"What are — ?"

"Shhh."

In the far distance, he could make out the muffled clomp of shod hooves.

"They are coming," said Li Mei thinly.

"Come on." Cuno gentled her over his shoulder and resumed his weaving course down the ridge.

The roan stood where he'd staked it near a spring nestled in a cottonwood grove, starlight gleaming in its hide like sequins. The horse whinnied when it heard Cuno and the girl coming, and reared, pulling against its rope. Cuno set the girl on the horse's back, behind the saddle, then grabbed the reins and climbed into the leather.

"Hold on tight, girl!" Cuno said. "We're

gonna ride like hell!"

He turned the horse away from the trees and ground his heels into its flanks. They bulled through brush, leapt a narrow creek, and headed south through the canyon, which he was only somewhat certain had an outlet. If he was wrong, the killers were going to have a high old time very soon, picking Cuno and Li Mei off like pintails on a back eddy . . .

As the horse rode haltingly through the brush and pines along the creek, the canyon walls leaned in, blocking out the stars. Cuno's heart fell. A box canyon.

Then they traced a long, gentle bend, and the pines opened, leaning back against the canyon walls. Not far beyond, a crack shone in the wall ahead, salted with flickering stars. The horse balked at the rocks crowding the canyon's back door. Cuno cooed to the mount, reining it this way and that, until they found a game path through the rubble.

After one final leap, with shod hooves clacking off stones and rocks tumbling behind, horse and riders were through the wall, tearing off down another, wider canyon on the other side.

They'd ridden ten minutes when shadows moved fifty yards ahead, starlight winking off metal. A man shouted, *"There!"*

Feeling the girl behind him draw a sharp breath, Cuno checked the roan down. "Shit." The canyon the killers had occupied must not have been a box canyon either.

He turned the horse as pistols popped behind him, and galloped back the way he'd come. Seconds later, he again hauled back on the reins.

More men were riding toward him — jostling silhouettes against the pine-enclosed game path. They had him surrounded, cut off.

Cuno jerked his head from left to right. Up the pine-covered hill to his left, a faint opening in the trees.

"Hold on, girl!"

She sucked another breath, tightened her arms about his waist, and pressed her cheek to his sweat-slick back as he neck-reined the horse right. In seconds, they were bounding up the knoll, the horse's hooves snapping branches, pistols and rifles cracking behind them, the slugs plunking into trees and spanging off rocks and buzzing like hornets about their ears.

The roan snorted, dug its hooves in as the grade steepened and the trail turned slightly right.

Cuno cast a quick glance over his left shoulder. The riders were keeping pace, pistols popping and stabbing orange flames into the darkness. A slug whipped so close to his right cheek that he could feel the slight, tingling burn as it continued past and zinged into the stone-floored trail rising before the horse's lunging front hooves.

"Keep your head down," he told Li Mei, turning his own head forward, kicking the roan's ribs, and whipping the rein ends against its hindquarters, urging more speed.

Behind him, growing louder, the killers yelled and whooped like demons, the hooves of their racing horses clacking over the hillside's exposed granite. They rode single file along the overgrown wagon trail, ducking under pine boughs protruding from the forest on both sides.

The trail forked. Avoiding bullets, Cuno followed the right fork, the horse climbing still higher.

Too high, too steep. They couldn't stay ahead of the gang at this pace.

On a slight, level shelf in the hillside, Cuno reined the horse to a skidding halt and slipped out of the saddle. He grabbed Li Mei in both arms, ripped her off the horse's back, her hair flying, the girl shrieking with shock.

Cuno had seen what looked like the frame of an old digging on the left. The cover was the only chance he and the girl had to hold the killers at bay.

Holding the girl's left arm, he slipped his Winchester from the horse's sheath, then rammed the butt against the roan's right hip. The roan gave an indignant whinny and galloped up the hill, stirrups batting its sides, shod hooves slipping on the slick, uneven stone.

Running, half-dragging the girl behind him, Cuno glanced back the way he'd come. The killers approached in a mass, triggering shots and shouting angry curses.

"They're on their feet!"

"Run 'em the fuck down."

"Damnit, I want that girl back. Whoever took her is gonna die *slow!*"

Cuno stopped, shoved the girl forward. "Run into that mine and get as far back as you can."

A bullet streaked past his face, chewing bark from the tree behind him. He rammed a shell into the Winchester's breech and dropped to a knee. He fired three quick rounds into the dark, shadowy horde approaching now within thirty yards.

Hearing more angry curses and the scream of a wounded horse, Cuno bolted forward through the pines. Ahead, the girl climbed the strewn mine tailings on her hands and knees. Once past the rubble, she turned into the timbered frame of the mine portal.

Cuno followed her, holding the Winchester in his right hand, his leather boot soles slipping along the strewn rocks and gravel, twisting his ankles. Falling, he cut his wrist, scrambled quickly to his feet, and continued lunging over the ore.

From what he could tell in the darkness, the tunnel was low but deep, and it dropped quickly into the hill. It smelled like minerals, gunpowder, and bat guano. Hearing the shouts of Cannady's men, he turned toward the forest beyond the tailings. Shadows moved toward him, spread out amongst the trees, often indistinguishable from the tree trunks. Several men fired toward the portal. Cuno knelt, snaked his Winchester around the frame, and, keying on the bursts of orange, let go several blue whistlers.

The shooting paused. The shadows dropped or scrambled for cover.

"Oh, God . . . oh, God. . . ." It was the girl behind him. When Cuno paused in his shooting to turn to her, she said in a quaking voice, "There's nowhere to go. We're trapped."

Cuno ejected a smoking shell, aimed at a moving shadow, and fired.

"Shit!" a man screeched, dropping down

behind a tree.

Cuno ejected that shell and levered a fresh one.

Watching the shadows spread out around him, he knew the girl was right. They had nowhere to go. Cuno probably had a dozen .44 shells in his pistol belt, maybe six .45s for the revolver. Doubtful there was a back door to the mine shaft.

The gang could simply wait them out.

One of the gang members seemed to be reading his mind.

"All you done is found a grave, you son of a bitch!" Laughter pitched the man's voice high. "Why don't you throw the girl out? No point in her dyin' when it ain't necessary. I was just gonna give her to a friend has a whorehouse to Sundance."

"Better she die of the clap than lead poisoning," another man called.

Several more shots rapped the weathered frame of the shaft, spraying slivers. Cuno and Li Mei moved back into the shaft and lay prone on the dusty, wooden floor strewn with rocks fallen from the ceiling.

Cuno returned fire, keeping the brow of the floor before him, which absorbed most of the hard cases' fusillade.

He'd just fired another round when, ejecting the casing, he glanced back at Li Mei cowering against the wall off his right shoulder.

"I reckon all I did was take you out of the frying pan and throw you into the fire. Maybe you best do what Cannady wants. Take your chances in Sundance."

"I will not," Li Mei said resolutely. "I will die here with you. The man who tried to save me."

"You'll be dying with a copper-riveted fool. I couldn't have dragged you into a worse situation if I'd tried."

The sentence had barely left his lips than the floor dropped an inch or so, the wood planks cracking beneath his weight.

Cuno's heart stopped. He held his breath, looking down. The planks hadn't been laid on solid ground. They'd been laid across a hole. The eerie screech and whine of ancient wood slowly giving beneath him assaulted his ears.

"Oh!" Li Mei cried.

"You know," Cuno said thinly, pushing slowly onto his elbows, "I might've spoke too soon." The wood cracked again, dropping farther. Cuno's voice rose as he threw an arm toward the girl. "Crawl on back away — !"

The floor opened up like a giant mouth, the wood cracking and the broken planks dropping with a great belching, thundering din.

Cuno heard Li Mei's shrill scream above the roar as he and the girl tumbled straight down into darkness.

18

Cannady looked up from the rock he'd dived behind, glanced above the mine rubble to the portal. Smoke billowed from the mouth, ghostlike in the darkness. The other men, having heard the rumble, had held fire.

Cannady glanced at Case Oddfellow and Ned Crockett, crouched behind a boulder to his left. "What the hell was that?"

"Sounded like a cave-in," said Case.

Cannady stared at the gaping mine portal, from which no more sounds issued.

"Hey, son of a bitch in the mine!" he shouted, cupping his hands around his mouth. "You still kickin'?"

Nothing.

"Let's check it out," said Ed Brown, standing behind a tree somewhere to Cannady's right.

"Hold on," Cannady ordered. "Might be a trap."

"Whinnie," yelled Brown, his deep voice booming amongst the trees, "go check it out!"

"I ain't checkin' it out. You check it out!"

"Goddamnit!" Brown shouted, his voice cracking with fury. "I done told you to check it out. You owe me two cartwheels. You check it out, I'll call us even."

Someone snickered. There was the metallic rasp of a rifle lever, the tinny clatter of a spent cartridge falling in gravel.

"Ah, shit," said Whinnie, stepping out of the trees left of Brown — a stocky, bulbous-gutted figure in high-topped boots and a high-crowned hat, holding an old-model rifle across his chest. "I'll check it out, goddamnit, but you sure as pig shit better call us even, or . . ."

"Or you'll *what?*"

"Shut up, both of ya," ordered Cannady. "Whinnie, haul your ass up there and see what the hell happened. Be quick about it. I'd still like to get a little shut-eye before dawn."

"All right, all right," complained Whinnie, crawling over the mine rubble, keeping his head raised toward the portal from which only silence issued. The dust had settled. The portal crouched across the rubble like a giant sleeping with his mouth open.

Whinnie spidered up the rocks and, breathing hard and staying low, edged a look through the mine mouth. He raised his rifle, sent several booming shots into the gaping, black hole. The shots ricocheted like firecrackers in a tin can.

Slowly, Whinnie straightened, staring intently at the mine floor.

Cannady chuffed. "Well, what the hell is it?"

A high-pitched chuckle sounded as the stocky man turned his head toward Cannady. "The floor done fell out from under 'em!"

Cannady stepped out from the tree. The others followed suit, and soon they'd all clambered over the rocks and stood outside the portal frame, staring into the cave. Like Whinnie had said, the floor had given way, the rotten planks dropping into another mine pit.

The men stood around the hole, snickering. Whinnie kicked a stone into the cavern. Two seconds later, the dull plop rose up through the darkness.

"Water," Whinnie observed. "Good fifty feet down."

Cannady dropped to one knee, canted his head over the hole. "Hey, son of a bitch — you alive down there?"

His voice echoed faintly before the hole swallowed it.

"Whoever he was," Case said, "he's dead now."

"The girl too," said Brown. "Sorry, Cannady. I know how you was wantin' to turn her over to that whorehouse, make amends with your cousin."

Cannady dug around in his shirt pocket, extracted a match. He raked the lucifer to life with his thumbnail and extended his arm into the hole.

The feeble light revealed only a foot-long stretch of the cavern walls, eight feet across, showing the chips and gouges of rock picks and shovels. Below lay darkness, thick as tar. The cool air wafting up smelled musty and humid. From deep inside the earth's bowels rose the faintly echoing screech of a rat.

"What a way to go." Cannady dropped the match and rose. "Well, just to make sure . . ." He canted the barrel of his Remington over the hole and loosed six shots, filling the cave mouth with the smell of cordite.

He spat into the hole, turned away, and, holstering the six-gun, stalked back the way he'd come. "One Chink's good as another, and I *will* find another." He yawned. "Don't know about you fellas, but I'm goin' back to sleep."

Deep in the hole, chest-deep in frigid ground water, Cuno dug his fingers into a cleft in the cave wall with his left hand while holding Li Mei around her waist with the other arm.

The girl shivered, teeth clattering. They both kicked their legs in the water as Cuno held them snug against the wall with his left hand. Apparently, the girl couldn't swim. Whenever he loosened his grip, she slipped straight down in the water, sucking air nervously and grabbing frantically at his shirt and belt, entangling her legs in his, threatening to drown them both.

He didn't know how deep the pit was. When he'd hit the water, he'd shot maybe twenty feet down without touching bottom.

This was obviously an old digging, possibly ancient. No doubt more recent prospectors had stumbled upon it and, nailing planks over the original hole, added another tunnel straight into the hill.

The old planks now floated in the stygian water around Cuno and Li Mei. Their faces sported the nicks and cuts from when the planks had fallen on them during their descent from above.

They'd managed to avoid getting pinked by Cannady's rifle shots by hugging a small alcove.

"Are they gone?" the girl asked in a pinched voice, which sounded sepulchral in the close quarters. The water chugged and gurgled around them, unseen.

"Sounds like."

Renewing his grip around her waist, Cuno ground his left hand deeper into the cleft. The hold wouldn't last much longer. His hand was getting so tired that the fingers felt as though nails had been driven through them.

"What do we do now?" the girl asked through a sob.

"Good question."

He looked around. The cave was black as the inside of a buried coffin. Occasionally, there was a dull flash off the water, vagrant starlight seeping in from above. Otherwise, there was no difference between his eyes being open or closed.

"Whoever dug this pit had to have a way down here."

Cuno felt around for a lower handhold — one that Li Mei could grasp. Finding one, he guided the girl's small, shaking hand to it, then found another notch she could rest her foot on, taking some of the strain off the hand.

Leaving her clinging awkwardly to the wall, her teeth clicking together, Cuno swam around the pit, running his hands against the wall, feeling for handholds. There were many pits and clefts, slight fissures probably caused by humidity over the years, but nothing like the steps he'd been hoping for. Whoever had dug the pit must have used ropes and pulleys to climb in and out and to remove the ore.

Shit.

He stopped and, growing heavy with fatigue, the water seemingly sucking him down into its black, chill depths, he looked around, opening his eyes wide as if to see better. It did no good.

The wall eight inches from his face was black velvet, unrelieved and undefined. Cuno moved ahead, kicking off the wall with his waterlogged boots, guiding with his left hand, using the right to tread water.

As he did so, his right hand touched something that didn't feel like wood planking. He gripped it, flipped it in his hand, running his thumb and index finger down its two-foot length — slender and smooth but knobbed at both ends.

Realizing it was a human bone, probably an arm or a leg, he dropped it, curling his lip. "Christ."

"What is it?" the girl asked in a quaking voice.

A prospector must have fallen into the pit before the planks had been laid. No reason for the girl to know that.

"Just in a foul mood's all."

"Oh." She swallowed. "Me too."

Cuno kicked himself forward. After another minute's search, his left hand found a knob of sorts, and gripped it. Using it to pull himself up, digging his boots against the wall, he found another about three feet above and right. He threw his left hand up, rammed his fingers into a cleft, and, gritting his teeth so hard he thought his jaws would crack, pulled.

His wet clothes and boots hung heavy, pulling him down. Water sluiced off him, raining into the pit. He should have kicked the boots off. Too late now. Though his bulging arms felt like rubber, he was making progress.

He reached up again with his right hand.

Damn . . . nothing but smooth stone only slightly relieved and gouged by pick blades and drills. He waved the right hand directly above his head.

There — another knob.

Reaching for it, he ground his left boot

into a crack.

The crack crumbled beneath his boot sole.

Cuno's left hand jerked out of its cleft, and he fell straight down the wall like a grain sack dropped from a barn mow.

Splash!

The cold water closed around him, ringing his ears. He fought to the surface, spitting water, arms flailing blindly for purchase. His left fist smacked the wall — the bark of skinned, bruised knuckles. Ignoring the pain, he grabbed the only crack he could find, grinding the tips of his fingers into it.

"Oh . . . God . . . I can't hold on. . . ." It was the girl, crying.

Spitting water and blinking, Cuno turned. "Li Mei."

Another splash as the girl hit the water, immediately gasping and flailing at the surface.

Cuno had no strength left. Still, he threw his right arm out. His hand found her head, then slipped down, and he wrapped his fingers around her arm. He pulled her to him. Doing so, he lost his grip on the wall, and he too bobbed in the water like a bottom-heavy cork, trying to keep the girl afloat with his numb right hand.

Finally, he found another handhold, and brusquely dragged the gagging girl toward him and grabbed her around the waist. He coughed up water and looked around, feeling as desperate as he'd ever felt. Even if he could find enough handholds to climb up the wall to freedom, he wouldn't have the strength.

The pit had him, and it wasn't letting go.

He held the girl close. She convulsed with anguished sobs, calling for her father as she shivered against Cuno. As hard as he gripped her, he felt his arm and hands weakening, the muscles failing from exhaustion. In his mind's eye, she slipped down his side, out away from him, sinking down in the black water.

He dug his fingers so deep into her side that she cried out in agony.

"Hold on," he told himself aloud. "Goddamnit, there's gotta be —"

"Li Mei! Cuno!"

The accented voice rang from above, echoing tonelessly off the pit's walls. At first, Cuno wasn't sure it wasn't his imagination or merely the water and wood gurgling around his legs.

"Papa!" Li Mei cried thinly. "We're *here!*"

Cuno followed the girl's gaze straight up the pit. There the darkness was less solid, more murky. He saw nothing. But the voice that cut through the murk was Kong's.

"I am here. Is Cuno with you?"

Cuno tightened his grip on the knob, which had become slick from his scraped, bloody fingers. "I'm here! Throw a rope!"

Time slowed down, and Cuno's muscles turned to lead as Kong, finding that his own rope wasn't long enough, had to retrieve Cuno's roan and splice Cuno's rope to his own. When Cuno finally heard the end of the rope slap the water, he was nearly too weak to grab it and hold his head above the water as he slipknotted the rope around Li Mei's waist.

Kong pulled the girl up easily, while Cuno clung to a knob with both bloody hands, wedging the edge of one boot sole into a crack. Gritting his teeth, he pressed his forehead against the wet wall and summoned all remaining strength to his arms and the foot braced against the crack.

Below, the pit was a huge viper mouth sucking him down.

After what seemed a miserably long time, Kong called, "I drop rope to you now, Cuno!"

The hemp whistled through the darkness to his right. He threw out his right hand, grabbed it, awkwardly knotted the end around his waist with numb, bloody fingers, and yelled for Kong to pull.

Two seconds later, Cuno rose with a jerk. The air squeezed from his lungs as he was slammed against the wall, then pulled straight up against it before he could get his heavy boots out before him. He walked up the side as the horse pulled, water sluicing out his boot tops and running back up his legs to his knees.

He shivered uncontrollably from the cold water and exhaustion.

Though every bone and muscle in his body cried out in pain, he'd never felt such deep relief as when his head broke over the pit's rim and the horse dragged him onto the mine's stony outer ledge.

"Ho, horse!" Kong yelled.

Cuno turned onto his side and, breathing hard and snaking his fingers under the rope to slacken it, lifted his gaze. Kong knelt before him, one hand on Cuno's shoulder.

"You okay?" the Chinaman asked.

"Am I alive?"

"I borrow horse from whores, follow you. Lucky for you I did. Lost your trail for a while, but found it again."

Cuno was too tired and sore to do anything but nod.

"Li Mei!"

Cuno snapped his eyes open again to see Kong bound off behind him. He rolled over to his other side. Li Mei sat with her back to the cave's outside wall, head resting against the wooden frame. She wasn't moving. Kong dropped to a knee, pressed an ear to the girl's chest.

He grabbed her arm. "Li Mei!"

The girl lifted her head slightly and groaned as she jerked the arm away.

Kong moved the arm out before her to inspect it. Slowly, he turned his head to Cuno. His voice was low and thick with shock. "My daughter shot!"

19

Cuno stood heavily. His steps faltering and wet boots squeaking, he walked over and knelt down beside Kong. The Chinaman was talking to his daughter, lightly shaking her, getting no response except groans.

"Let me see." Cuno nudged Kong aside and took the girl's arm gently in his hands, inspecting the bloody, wet hole in her shirt, about three inches above her elbow.

With his bowie knife, he made a long cut up the sleeve, then peeled the wet wool back from the small, round bullet hole. The slug had entered through the back of her arm, exiting the front. It didn't appear to have hit the bone.

No doubt she'd been shot when she and Cuno were trying to elude Cannady's jackals. Hadn't said anything. Tough girl.

With two deft knife slashes, Cuno cut the sleeve entirely off her arm, then sheathed his knife and began wrapping the cloth around the arm, knotting it taut over the hole, ignoring the girl's groaning protests.

"Gotta get her warm."

Kong nodded. "You too."

Cuno looked around. His roan and Kong's steeldust, which Cuno remembered from the Heaven's Bane stables, stood left of the rubble, head-to-head, reins dangling.

Cuno picked up the girl and pushed himself to his feet. He tripped over his boot toes as he staggered toward the horses. When Kong had climbed into the steeldust's saddle, Cuno lifted the girl up to him. He couldn't keep his teeth from clacking as he shivered.

"We'll head for cover and build a fire."

He grabbed the roan's reins and climbed heavily into the saddle, booted the gelding down the hill toward the valley bottom. He wasn't aware of much after that, but went through the motions of finding a hidden hollow in the darkness, unsaddling his horse, building a fire, and throwing out his bedroll as if sleepwalking. He stripped quickly, lay down beside the fire, wrapped himself in his blankets, and went to sleep.

There was a long, luxurious blackness. As if in the far distance, he heard someone moving around, heard twigs snapping and the dull thuds of an ax driven into wood.

When he opened his eyes, his lids were heavy and sticky. For a second, he thought he'd been buried alive. He looked down his chest. Several ratty blankets and a shaggy, musty deerskin had been piled atop his own army blankets. The heavy covers and the fire popping and cracking somewhere near his feet made him feel mummified.

The air was rife with the succulent smell of roasting meat, making Cuno's mouth water.

Five feet above his head, an awning of spruce limbs had been erected, lean-to fashion, over willow poles bound with rawhide.

Spying movement to his left, Cuno turned his head. Kong squatted over Li Mei, who slept under a pile of covers much like Cuno's. The Chinaman was running a wet cloth down the girl's flushed, glistening forehead. He met Cuno's gaze.

"Found blankets in abandon trapper cabin. Killed deer." The Chinaman wrung out the cloth in the pan. "How you feel?"

Cuno swallowed, looked outside the lean-to. A few feet away lay the cook fire over which a venison haunch roasted on a braided willow spit. Cuno's coffeepot chugged and sputtered on a flat rock in the coals.

Over the small hollow surrounded by a tangle of brush, evergreens, and boulders, the sky was soft gray. It was either early morning or early evening. The lack of dew in the brush indicated the latter. Chill air pushed against him from both sides while the fire bathed him with heat, filled his nostrils with the rich, succulent aroma of the meat.

"How long I been asleep?"

"Nearly whole day. Li Mei too. She sweats from fever, in and out of sleep." Kong sponged the girl's right cheek, lines of concern in his face. His voice was soft. "I worry."

Cuno rose to a sitting position, lifted his hands to finger the bandage around his head, where the lookout's rifle slug had creased his skull. Kong must have dressed the wound while Cuno slept.

His brain felt heavy and he realized, sitting up and looking around, the small encampment pitching gently from side to side, that the slug had addled him more than he'd thought during his and the girl's run. His weak limbs told him he'd lost a good bit of blood too.

They'd have to get the girl to Sundance tomorrow, find a doctor. Cuno would guide them. No telling how Kong and Li Mei might be received. Without the proper urging, a white doctor might not treat a Chinese.

Cuno said as much to Kong as he flipped all the blankets aside but one.

"What about Mr. Parker?" Kong asked.

"He'll have to bring the team on alone." Cuno wrapped the blanket around his naked waist and stood heavily, staggering, and padded across the pine cones and gravel to the right side of the hollow.

Pissing on a juniper shrub, he glanced over his left shoulder. "Once I get you two situated in town, I'll see to the Cannady wolves. If they haven't robbed the bank already, maybe I can throw a wrench into their wheel spokes."

Finished with his business, he wrapped the blanket tight around his waist and stumbled back to the lean-to. The cool air felt good against his chest, sweaty from the fire-warmed robes.

Kong glanced at Cuno, who was using a leather swatch to remove the blackened coffeepot from the fire. "They are very bad men. Too bad for just one man."

Cuno poured the smoking coffee into a battered tin cup, tore off a chunk of meat from the haunch roasting on the spit. He bit off some of the meat and chewed as he stared into the fire, hearing the revolver pop as Cannady blew lead through Wade's forehead.

"You worry about your daughter." He swallowed the meat, chased it with hot coffee. "I'll worry about Cannady's bunch."

Cuno and Kong were up the next morning well ahead of the sun in this deep mountain hollow, cold and swathed in fog.

Bundled in their heavy coats, they washed more of the venison haunch down with hot coffee and corn cakes, which Kong had cooked the night before, then saddled up and broke camp. Kong eased the blanket-wrapped, half-conscious Li Mei onto his saddle, then crawled up behind her.

They were on the trail a good hour before the fog finally lifted and a cobalt sky shone above the pine-mantled, hawk-hunted ridges. An hour after that, the town of Sundance appeared on a craggy, bald, saffron ridge high above the tree line. From a mile out and two hundred yards below, the swaybacked village looked like a giant anthill, with the heavy mountain ore wagons and horseback riders milling amongst the rocks and scarps below and on both sides being the ants.

Rough wooden buildings formed a rickety

line atop the ridge, the makeshift structures rammed together like battered, multicolored dominoes ready to be swept into the rocky gorge below at the first blast of a November snow squall. The town was a mile away, but it looked improbably close and detailed under the clear, white light of the high-country sun. Three mongrel dogs fought over refuse on the slope below the town, two snarling angrily while the third — a pup — sat back and howled. The dogs' sparring and the metronomic pounding of an unseen stamping mill carried as clearly as a throat clearing in a hushed cathedral.

Cuno, Kong, and Li Mei followed the switchbacks into the town, where the chill wind rattled the shingle chains and made the rickety buildings squawk and lean to the south. They made their way around wagons as well as pedestrians, dogs, and chickens into the heart of the raucous village. Sundance was typical of mining camps in that every other building was either a saloon or a brothel or both, and every other woman was painted and proudly displaying her wares from a balcony overlooking the main trace.

Cuno turned his roan toward a hitch rack before a hotel he'd patronized on previous trips. It was painted bright green, and the huge letters over the roofed stoop identified it as the EVERGREEN INN. There were better places in town, but during his last two visits he hadn't awakened to more than one or two bedbug bites, and the rats ran mostly only on the first floor. The miners' famous shovel fights usually occurred over at the Mother Lode on the other end of town, and whores tended to shun the place because the owner was a lay minister from Iowa.

Just the place for Li Mei to recuperate from her bullet wound.

Carrying the blanketed girl in his arms, Kong followed Cuno inside. The freighter paused at the front desk, where the pious, fat-faced owner, whose name he couldn't recall, was scribbling a letter on a lined notepad, sticking his pudgy tongue out the right corner of his mouth with concentration. His round, gold spectacles hung low on his chubby nose, which was impossibly white for being so close to the sun here in Sundance.

As the clock ticked loudly onto the papered wall behind him, Cuno flipped several coins on the man's notepad. "Two rooms. Not sure when we're leavin', but I'll pay three days in advance."

The man — Cuno just remembered that his name was Carl Miller — looked up with a pleasant smile. He nudged his glasses up his nose with an ink-stained forefinger. His mild blue eyes found Kong and the girl, and the corners of his mouth turned down. He swept the coins from his pad with a quick flick of the hand that held the pen.

"I'm sorry." He glanced at a chalked sign hanging from a nail beneath the stairs. "No Indians, niggers, Jews, Poles, dogs, pigs, or Mongolians. I'll accept Prussians, but they must bathe elsewhere *first.*"

He dipped his pen and returned his attention to his notepad.

Cuno unsheathed his revolver. He clicked the hammer back. As Miller jerked his head up at the sound, Cuno planted the end of the barrel against the hotel proprietor's forehead, shoving him straight back in his chair. The man dropped his pen and threw his hands up, grunting and crossing his eyes as he stared at the Colt in Cuno's clenched fist.

Cuno gritted his teeth. "You're gonna make an exception for these two *Mongolians,* aren't you?"

The man gasped, swallowed, and nodded his head.

"You're not going to tell anyone about us . . . are you?"

The man shook his head quickly.

"And you're going to waddle your fat ass across the street and fetch the sawbones pronto . . . aren't you?"

The man swallowed again, flexed the fingers of both hands. He was breathing hard. Sweat was popping out on his forehead as his voice quaked, "Yes . . . yes, I suppose I can do that."

Cuno lowered the pistol but kept it cocked and aimed at Miller. "Now, why don't you hand over a couple keys and get on about your errands?"

A few minutes later, Kong carried Li Mei up to their second-floor room while Cuno stabled the two horses in the livery barn. When he was making the second and final trip back to the hotel with their gear, he heard the doctor speaking inside Kong's room. The tone was administering, even gentle. Not belligerent, as Cuno had expected.

The freighter went into his own room next to Kong's, and stretched out on the bed.

He'd have a smoke and a glass of water, then head out looking for Cannady's clan and ponder the problem of taking them all down without taking himself down as well.

He hadn't been on the bed long, however, before his eyes grew heavy. The cold water and the blood loss. Damn.

He mashed out his cigarette and scuttled down on the bed.

He'd doze just a bit. . . .

He didn't how much time had passed when he opened his eyes and looked up from his pillow. The room was dark but for the flickering torchlight angling in his street-side window. There was no longer much wagon traffic, and the voices on the street were raucous, at once angry and jubilant.

It was late enough that the miners were getting well into their cups. Another hour, and the shovel fights would start. . . .

Cuno set one boot on the floor, then froze.

Shambling footsteps in the hall. They stopped outside Cuno's room. Someone knocked — three soft taps.

Cuno grabbed his .45, ratcheted back the hammer.

"Who is it?"

The raspy male voice on the other side of the door betrayed a Scotch accent. "Message from a lady, sir."

Cuno frowned. He didn't know any ladies in Sundance.

"You must have the wrong room."

"Not if you're Cuno Massey." The man pitched his voice low with irony and gravity. The slurred words betrayed a libation or two. "The lady — and a fine-lookin' lass she is too — wants to see ye in her room at the Periwinkle."

20

Cuno climbed off the bed and opened the door, aiming his pistol at the fat belly of the man standing on the other side of the threshold.

He was a ratty, unshaven gent in a wool coat several sizes too small, with grizzled pewter-brown hair falling from a soiled derby hat sporting two bullet holes. He hadn't shaved in several days. He smelled like cheap tobacco, piss, whiskey, hay, and rancid sweat.

He wasn't wearing a gun. At least, not on the outside. Nevertheless, Cuno kept the Colt aimed at the man's hairy gut peering out from his soiled plaid vest and two open shirt buttons.

"Hey, hey!" the man complained. "No need for that. I'm doin' you a favor, bub."

Cuno glanced up and down the dark hall. Cannady or one of the jackal's men might have seen him, Kong, and the girl ride into town, and set a trap. "I don't know any women in this burg, mister. You'd best drift."

"Miss Glory says you do." He grinned broadly, flashing tobacco-stained teeth.

"Glory?" It took a few seconds to cast the name up from his memory. "The only Glory I know is a sporting girl in Julesburg."

"I think you'll be pleased to find she ain't no longer in Julesburg. A sportin' girl still, but she's workin' over to the Periwinkle now. And ain't you the lucky one — her clearin' her busy schedule for you and you alone this magnificent mountain eve!" The soiled Scot crooked a finger. "Follow me. You've been summoned."

Cuno stared after the man, who'd turned to stride toward the stairs.

What the hell was Glory doing in Sundance?

Last time Cuno had seen her — if this was indeed the same curvaceous blonde — she and her two colleagues, Minnie and Frieda, had helped him out of a tight spot with Franklin Evans. Cuno had killed Evans's son while saving Minnie's life a couple of years ago, in a sporting house in Julesburg.

The senior Evans had sicced bounty hunters after Cuno, and the bounty hunters

259

had killed July. Cuno had killed Evans, as well as the most formidable bounty hunter of all, Ruben Pacheca, at Evans's own ranch.

That had been two years ago. . . .

"Come on, mate," called the Scot from the top of the stairs. "No man keeps a girl like Miss Glory waitin'!"

Cuno grumbled, turned around, and grabbed his hat. He didn't have time for sporting girls — even one as bewitching as Miss Glory — but it wouldn't be polite to turn down her summons. She must have seen him ride into town earlier. He'd have a drink with her, then get on about his business of avenging Wade Scanlon.

Donning his hat and closing the door, he hitched his .45 high on his hip, and followed the aromatic messenger downstairs and outside.

Firebrands lit up the saloons like the smoking gates of hell. Out-of-tune piano music served as background for the raucous din of miners drinking, singing, gambling, arguing, or fighting over whores.

The street was jammed with foot traffic as the men wandered between saloons, drinks in their fists, cigarettes or cigars in their teeth, some with gaudily dressed and painted women on their arms. The women were as drunk as the miners, and just as foul. A few horseback riders tried to make their way through the crowd, several hazing the drunk miners out of their path with their hats or quirts.

As the Scot led Cuno past an alley mouth, Cuno saw three prospectors fighting over a bruised, bare-breasted girl crouched against a rain barrel and screaming at the prospectors in one of the Scandinavian tongues. Cuno and the Scot crossed the street, angling toward a narrow, three-story building knocked together out of pine planks and shake shingles.

The hovel looked like a Nebraska farmhouse with an extra story, but was listing to one side despite its recent construction. Firebrands burned on three of the four porch posts, lighting the large sign announcing PERIWINKLE, the word abutted on both sides with "Girls" written in flowing curlicues of pitch-black paint.

In the guttering torchlight, Cuno saw that the place was aptly named, for, excepting the sign, it was painted periwinkle blue from roofline to foundation.

He also saw that several of the men milling around the porch with girls on their knees were some of the same men he'd seen in Cannady's camp two nights ago.

Heart skipping a beat, he paused on the

261

front step, staring at one of the men — a big black man dressed in black with a blue neckerchief, who laughed and bounced a young redhead, naked except for a broad-brimmed black hat and a pair of men's black boots, up and down on his knee. He didn't look at Cuno. Two of the others gave him a belligerent passing glance, then turned away.

Cuno took a slow, deep breath and followed the Scot through the open front door and into a small foyer, through a sitting room area that also boasted a bar and in which several more men flirted with naked or half-naked, feather-haired women. A midget in child-sized dungarees and with an enormous red nose played a fiddle while a lone couple danced, clapping their hands.

Cuno strode past a gambling room, then, spying a familiar face in the next room, paused before the door.

One of the men inside — with a scruffy beard, milky eye, and a green hummingbird tattooed on his cheek — fit the description that Serenity Parker had provided of Clayton Cannady himself. Playing poker with Cannady were several other obvious killers and two men wearing deputy sheriff stars.

"Pssst!"

Cuno looked ahead. The Scot was on a

staircase, three steps up, leaning over the rail and beckoning. "Right this way to heaven, me laddie!"

Cuno doubted that. His heart was thumping irregularly and his hands were sweaty. He wished he had the Winchester rifle he'd lost in the flooded mine. Brushing a hand across the grips of his revolver, he continued ahead and up the stairs.

The second story was carpeted in blue rugs, with blue wallpaper and blue bracket lamps. The Scot tapped twice on a door on the hall's left side with a crack on the upper panel, as if a man had tried to put his fist through it.

All around rose the sounds of fornication — moaning, groaning, sighing, and squawking bedsprings. Deep laughter rose from one of the rooms. The burnt-molasses smell of opium hung heavy in the hall's musty air.

The door opened. Cuno stared over the Scotchman's right shoulder. The heart-shaped face that peered back at him was indeed the lovely Glory's. Her full, red lips quirked a smile, blue eyes flashing.

"Brought him on the double, Miss Glory. You were right — he needed a little coaxin'. Suspicious lad. But here he is." The Scot hesitated, shifting his weight from one foot to the other, clearing his throat.

"That's the one, all right," Glory said, her eyes again flicking to Cuno. She plucked a rolled bill from her ample bosom, the corset shoving up both creamy mounds high and proud, her nipples pushing at the taut, white satin. "There you are, Simon. Go and have a nice time."

"Obliged, Miss Glory. Any time!" Squeezing the bill in his withered fist, Simon wheeled, gave Cuno a conspiratorial wink, and trotted back toward the stairs.

Glory regarded him bemusedly for a moment, her rich, tawny-blond hair piled atop her head, ringlets hanging down on both sides of her lightly rouged face. The room was dimly lit with blue and soft red lamplight, outlining her from behind, revealing the fact that she wore very little except the corset beneath her sheer, pale wrapper with its lace and puffed sleeves.

The wrapper was open, revealing bare thighs and flat belly. Her figure was as full-busted, round-hipped, and thin-wasted as Cuno remembered it. He remembered too the small, diamond-shaped birthmark two inches beneath her corset, under her right breast.

She smelled like talcum and sassafras.

Delectable. Instantly, primally alluring.

Cuno removed his hat and held her gaze.

264

She drew the door wide and stepped back into the room.

"Won't you come in?"

"I reckon that's why I'm here."

When he was in the room, she closed the door and threw herself into his arms, kissing him and flinging her arms around his back. She kissed him for a long time, breathing hard, running her hands across his shoulders. She pulled his head down and kissed the bandage. Finally, she slid her lips to his cheek, her breath warm and wet on his skin.

"It's so good to see you again, Cuno. When I saw you ride into town, I couldn't believe it was you."

She stepped back, smiling, holding his hands lightly in hers, her chin dipped seductively.

Cuno shook his head, which was swimming from the girl's heartfelt kiss and no longer aching. "You are something else, Miss Glory. And a sight for these sore eyes." He frowned. "What brought you to Sundance?"

"Work." She shrugged. "There was another shooting in Roderick's place in Julesburg, and the sheriff shut us down. Frieda, Minnie, and I had to take work where we could. Minnie went to Denver, Frieda to

Pueblo. I had a chance to come here. Couldn't turn down boomtown money."

Still holding his hands, she slid her lips back from her white teeth and beamed up at him. "And you? What are you doing in this godforsaken town, Cuno Massey? And what did you do to your poor head?"

"Started out haulin' boomtown supplies from Denver. Ended up tracking men."

"What men?"

"The men downstairs."

She turned suddenly, the wrapper billowing out around her long, naked legs. She strode toward a settee against the far wall. Halfway there, she turned back to him, beetling her brows. "What men are you talking about?"

"I only recognized a few. A big black man is one. Another is a man named Clayton Cannady, the group's ramrod. Has a hummingbird tattooed on his cheek, beneath his blind left eye." Cuno tossed his hat on the settee and sat down beside Glory. "They killed my partner, Wade Scanlon, a one-legged man — a *good* man — for sport."

"That's *terrible.*"

"You know 'em?"

"Cannady? I don't think so. But so many gun wolves pass through here, Sundance bein' a boomtown and all. What else do you

266

know about them?"

"I know they're here to rob a bank. I know they're downstairs right now in one of the gambling rooms, playing poker with a couple of deputy sheriffs."

She pursed her lips with disapproval. "Deputies, eh?"

"That tell you something?"

She grabbed his hand in both of hers. "Cuno, the sheriff died of food poisoning three days ago. Two days before, two other deputies rode out after claim jumpers. They haven't been seen since."

Cuno looked at her hands on his. "And the only two remaining lawmen are cavorting with killers." He smiled. "Sounds like someone's been tidyin' up the place." He ran a hand through his long, blond hair, flipping it out over his collar. "Gettin' ready for a bank robbery."

"When?"

Cuno shook his head.

She placed her hands on his left thigh and gazed up at him anxiously. "You're not going to try and stop them, are you? If they're the bunch I saw ride in yesterday, there's a whole passel of 'em. I know how big and strong and good with a gun you are, Cuno Massey, but you're only *one* man."

"That might be true." Cuno grabbed his

hat. "But I've got to do something. And there's no time like the present."

He started to stand, but she grabbed his arm, pulling him back down. "No!"

"Miss Glory, I 'preciate your —"

She pressed a finger to his lips, stared beseechingly into his eyes. "At least have a drink with me before you go?"

Cuno chuffed.

Glory pooched her lips in a pout. "For old times' sake?"

Cuno chuffed again and sagged back onto the settee. "Never could say no to you or Minnie or Frieda. What is it with you girls anyway?"

Chuckling, Glory stood and walked over to a long dressing table littered with female accoutrements including gewgaws and small silver boxes and perfume bottles. A liquor bottle and three goblets stood amidst the debris. With her back to him, Glory uncorked the bottle, filled two glasses, and strode back toward Cuno, moving seductively, offering a lopsided grin. Her bare feet softly slapped the bare floor before reaching the carpet upon which the settee sat.

"Might have something to do with how well we bandaged all those wounds you're so prone to acquiring."

Cuno remembered waking to Glory,

Frieda, and Minnie tending him in a feather bed, more naked than clothed and kneeling around him like he was some god dropped from Valhalla. Watching Glory sit down beside him now, her breasts pushing up out of her corset as she leaned against him and crossed her legs, one bare foot nudging his boot, he knew a sweet, lingering pang of desire.

"Brandy all right?" she asked, extending the glass.

"Brandy'll do." He took the glass and sipped, savored the fiery, pleasantly fruity liquid trickling down his throat and into his chest, warming his core. He looked into the glass, swirled it. "Good stuff."

"I know you're a whiskey man, but I had it sent up just for you. Thought I'd try to broaden your horizons."

He took another long drink. He hadn't realized how the chill of the flooded mine had lingered deep in his bones. "I appreciate that."

Glory was half turned to him, her breasts only inches from his chest. She ran a finger around the rim of her goblet, dipped it into the brandy, licked it off, then touched the finger to his cheek.

"I've been with a lot of men, but I've never enjoyed any man like I've enjoyed you." She canted her head slightly, her blue eyes glistening in the intimate lamplight. "Stay with me tonight?"

His chest felt heavy, and his head began swimming once more. It took him a few seconds to find his voice. "I really can't, Miss Glory. You know why —"

She moved against him, tipped his brandy glass to his lips. He drank. When he pulled the glass back down, she closed her full, wet lips over his. She kissed him for nearly a minute as she ran her hand slowly up his right thigh, pressing her heaving breasts against his chest. She pulled away, and her eyes slightly crossed as they gazed into his.

"Sure I can't change your mind?"

While kissing him, she'd untied her corset. It had fallen down to her waist, leaving her breasts bare. They were large and pear-shaped, still marked by the corset, with erect pink nipples, the soft creamy skin glistening with desire.

Her hand slid over his leg and inside his thigh, pressing against the denim. His head spun. For a minute, there were two Glorys. The brandy had set a fire inside him. His heart pounded, and his desire raged.

He wet his lips with his tongue. "I . . . uh . . . reckon I could stay for a little while."

He lowered his head to her breasts, ran his

tongue over each nipple for a long time before, breathing hard, she stood and removed her corset and wrapper.

He sat back against the settee, sipping his brandy and enjoying the warm, womblike feeling of the liquor and the soft blue and umber light and the beautiful woman standing before him naked, nipples jutting from her heavy breasts. She reached up to unpin her hair, let it billow like silk about her shoulders.

Then she knelt between his knees, unbuckled his pistol belt, opened his pants, and tugged them down his legs. When the pants and boots were off and cast away like debris, she smiled up at him smokily, lowered her head to his crotch, caressed his naked thighs with her fingernails, and closed her lips over his swollen member.

It wasn't until they were both naked in bed, and she was straddling him, throwing her head back on her shoulders as her body convulsed with rapture, that he realized he wasn't just drunk. He'd been drugged.

He lifted his head, his eyes rolling around in their sockets. He squinted as he tried to focus on only one of the three Glorys crying out in ecstasy atop him.

His voice sounded slurred and faraway even to his own ears. "What . . . was in . . .

that . . . brandy?"

She'd frozen with her head thrown back on her shoulders, her hair hanging straight down, wisping against his thighs. Now she lowered her gaze to his, and her eyes became pinched with sorrow. She crouched over him, cupping her hands over his ears.

"I slipped you a drug, you big, stubborn idiot."

He tried to frown, but he didn't have even that much control of his body. He lay limp beneath her. "Why?"

She kissed his cheek and stared into his eyes. Tears dribbled down her smooth cheeks. "Cuno, I've thrown in with the men you're after!"

She dropped her head to his chest, sobbing.

Cuno tried to push up on his elbows, but a second later he was out like a blown lamp.

21

Glory washed her face, pinned up her hair, and threw a heavy robe around her shoulders. She walked to the door of her room and glanced back at Cuno stretched out on the bed. She'd drawn the covers up to his chin. His chest rose and fell regularly as he slept.

She studied him for a time, her face drawn, then went out and, closing the door behind her, gathered the robe taut about her waist and moved languidly down the stairs to the bar.

The din of revelry rose around her, the tobacco smoke so thick she could barely breathe. As she moved around the chairs and tables and outstretched boots, someone grabbed her robe from behind. "Come on, Glory, park it on ole Chris's knee!"

Automatically turning on the practiced charm, Glory wheeled, grinning. "Chris, you incorrigible old mossy-horn — keep your hands to yourself. I'm done booked up fer tonight!" She leaned down and pecked the grizzled cheek. "Get here early tomorrow." She winked and turned away.

As Chris laughed behind her, admiring her ass through the robe, she strode across the saloon and poked her head into the gambling room in which Case Oddfellow, Clayton Cannady, and the two "deputies" played poker with three of Cannady's firebrands and two Irish prospectors.

Apparently, Case was letting the prospectors win for the time being. The weathered, bearded rock pickers appeared happy as pigs at breakfast, laughing raucously and slapping each other on the back as their eyes danced behind the smoke from the expensive cigars jutting from their rotten teeth.

Soon, when the rock breakers had taken a few more pulls from their bottle, Case would be dropping cards from his shirt cuffs and from under his hat, and dealing from the bottom of the deck. All the while, he'd be snickering with Cannady sitting to his right.

The miners would leave the table crestfallen, drunk, and fleeced.

"Willie! Alfred!" Glory called, cupping her hands around her mouth to yell above the roar.

When the two "deputies" looked at her through the billowing smoke, frowning, Glory canted her head back, beckoning.

"What is it, Glory?" Case asked. They were between hands, and the handsome Oddfellow was relaxing in his chair, lighting a long Mexican cheroot, puffing smoke from a corner of his mouth. His thick, black hair was combed straight back on his head.

"Little fracas upstairs," Glory called. "Nothin' our two *lawmen* can't handle."

Willie and Alfred, both dressed in shabby suits with soiled hats and deputy stars pinned to their shirts, glanced at Oddfellow. Case shrugged and canted his head toward Glory.

Grimacing with annoyance, Willie and Alfred reluctantly gained their feet. Alfred scratched his thin gray beard and threw back his shot glass, then looped his sawed-off shotgun over his shoulder and headed for Glory waiting in the doorway.

"You know, Miss Glory," Willie said, keeping his voice down so the townsmen and miners couldn't hear, "we ain't *really* lawmen. That was just our little charade hereabouts." He was a full head shorter than Alfred, with mean, close-set eyes and a purple birthmark sprayed across his pitted right temple. Glory recoiled from his breath,

275

which smelled like beer and chicken liver.

"You're in luck," Glory raked out through a sneer. "I don't need lawmen, just errand boys."

She wheeled haughtily and, Willie and Alfred following with indignant expressions, headed back up the stairs and down the hall to her room. She threw the door open and stepped inside. She looked at Cuno, still unconscious on the bed.

As Willie and Alfred shuffled into the room, Glory crossed her arms on her breasts and kept her haughty gaze on Cuno. "Haul him off to the jail and lock him up. Keep a quilt over him." She began gathering his clothes and boots from the floor. "Take these . . . and his gun. Make sure he can't get at the gun till he's out of the cell."

Alfred said, "What's this about, Miss Glory? He cause trouble?"

"He's an old friend," Glory said, shoving Cuno's clothes into Alfred's arms. "He's figured out what we're up to. I want him locked up so he doesn't get hurt." Her eyes sharpened. "Make sure he isn't hurt!"

The two men shared a skeptical glance. Willie sighed and reached for Cuno's left arm, grumbling, "Whatever you say, Miss Glory."

"Take him down the back stairs, and no

word of this to any of the others."

Pulling Cuno's unconscious, quilt-shrouded bulk over his shoulder and grunting with the effort, Willie cursed and turned toward the door. "Whatever you say, Miss Glory . . ."

Willie went out with Cuno and, with the freighter's clothes, boots, and cartridge belt in his arms and casting Glory an uncertain look, Alfred followed him.

Glory closed the door and stared at it, lips pooched out. Finally, she balled her fist and ran it against the cracked panel, then wheeled and flopped down on the bed, sobbing.

In the dank darkness, Cuno opened his eyes.

For a minute, he thought he was back in the flooded mine pit. But a cot was beneath him, and on top of him was a quilt.

He was shivering. The quilt gave little protection from the cold seeping through the barred window no larger than a shoe box in the mortared stone wall high above his head.

His skull ached sharply, as if a little man were inside, chipping away with a miniature pick. His mouth tasted foul. His brain was even foggier than before. The aftereffects of some drug or herb Glory had slipped into his brandy.

Glory.

Last night.

"Cuno, I've thrown in with the men you're after!"

Cuno's lip curled angrily and he pushed up on his elbows. "Stupid bitch."

In the darkness before him, a barred door. Bars to either side, glistening faintly in the stray light. Beyond the door, the main office of the jail. He couldn't see much but a few hulking shadows in the darkness. No sounds but the soft rustle of the chill breeze filtering through the barred window slot.

He must be alone in the jailhouse.

Unguarded.

Enraged and feeling stupid at having let himself be seduced and betrayed, he clambered off the squeaking, iron-framed cot and padded barefoot to the door. He curled his fingers around the bars, then pushed against them, straining his forearms, and pulled back.

There wasn't an ounce of give. The iron lock held fast.

The jailhouse was typical of those in most mining camps — crudely, stoutly constructed. The outlaws had left no guards because they knew no one could escape the place — at least, not without a shovel or a file.

Cuno stood naked, skin prickling at the cold air swirling off the stone walls, staring into the office shadows. He squeezed the bars and gritted his teeth.

Wheeling suddenly, he moved to the opposite wall, grabbed the window ledge, pulled himself up, and peered through the narrow slot. Beyond the stout stone wall was a dark alley, the wind shepherding trash along the ground. Ahead and right, a privy, its door banging softly in the breeze.

"Hey!" he shouted. "Anyone out there?"

His voice boomeranged back to echo around the cell. He released his fingers, dropped to the floor. Even if someone had heard, no one was going to let a prisoner out of jail — even if they knew it was Cannady's men who'd put him here.

Goddamn Glory!

Cuno rubbed his hands together, chilled to the bone. His clothes had been thrown onto the floor beside the cot. Reaching down, he grabbed the longhandles and began dressing. When he was finished, his shirt buttoned to his throat, he wrapped the quilt around his shoulders and sat at the edge of the cot, considering his options.

The floor lightened, gaining definition, as

the dawn seeped through the window. The breeze gentled. The smell of cook fires drifted into the cell.

The light gave the office beyond the cell more details. Cuno's gun belt was coiled atop a filing cabinet, twelve feet away. He stared at the gun as if to will it to him.

No way to get to it.

Outside, a rumbling sounded, growing louder, like a drumroll. Trace chains jangled and hooves clomped. A wagon was approaching the jailhouse.

Cuno stared out the office's single window, left of the door. There was no shade or curtain over it. The wagon appeared — a large, square contraption drawn by a six-horse team.

Two men sat in the box, one driving, one holding a double-barreled shotgun. Both burly, red-faced men were decked out in blue uniforms with leather-billed hats and high, black boots. It passed so quickly it was hard to be sure, but Cuno could have sworn the wagon was all iron.

Then he remembered that the wagon the local mine used to shuttle its ore from the town bank to the railhead on the eastern plains was an all-iron, steel-riveted beast called the Hell Wagon. The armored vehicle was impossible to bust into without a hundred pounds of dynamite. Four Pinkerton agents rode inside, armed with repeating rifles and sawed-off shotguns.

Cuno pricked his ears as he heard the driver halt the team in front of the mine-owned bank down the street. Knowing the Hell Wagon's reputation for impregnability, Cannady was no doubt going to hit the guards as they transferred the strongbox from the bank to the wagon.

Cuno squeezed the bars, stared out the window at the dim, vacant street and the closed shops beyond.

A dark, slender figure stepped before the window. The man turned to the jailhouse and peered inside, cupping his hands around his eyes.

Cuno's heart leapt. *"Kong!"*

The Chinaman's voice was muffled by the glass. "Cuno?"

"Get me outta here!"

The sentence was punctuated by two sharp rifle reports. Kong jerked and turned to look toward the bank. Someone shouted. A fusillade broke out amidst yells and screams, the gunfire echoing around the street. Clanging barks rose as slugs bounced off the Hell Wagon.

Cuno pulled at the cell door in frustration. "Kong!"

Kong cast another edgy glance into the office, then ran to the door. "It locked!"

"Kick it in!"

Between the door's vertical planks, Kong's shadow jostled. The door shuddered as the Chinaman kicked it.

"Harder!" Cuno shouted as the angry bursts of gunfire continued up the street. "Put some muscle into it!"

Kong kicked the door twice more. It didn't budge.

"The window!" Cuno shouted.

The Chinaman scurried to the window, rammed his elbow through it. The glass clattered and fell in shards. With his coat sleeve, Kong rubbed the shards from the edges of the frame, then hoisted himself through, getting his foot caught on the ledge and tumbling down the wall and hitting his right shoulder on the floor.

Cuno looked down at him. "Look in the desk for the keys!"

Wincing, the Chinaman pushed himself to his feet and ran to the desk, favoring his right shoulder. He opened one of the drawers, glanced inside, then opened the one beneath it. He returned his gaze to the top drawer, reached in with one hand, rummaged around, and pulled out a ring and two keys.

Cuno extended a hand through the bars. "Hurry!"

Kong slapped the ring into Cuno's hand. After trying the first key in the lock, he tried the second. The latch clicked. Cuno pushed the door open.

Outside, the shooting was growing more sporadic. Men whooped victoriously. Horses whinnied and screamed.

Cuno grabbed his gun off the filing cabinet, and strapped it around his waist. He ran to the gun rack on the office's right wall, where the three rifles were secured with a padlock and chain. He opened the padlock with a key from the ring, tossed the ring into a corner, grabbed a repeater from the rack, and levered a round into the breech.

The earthen floor shook as something big and fast bounded back toward the jail.

Cuno cursed.

The bastards had taken the gold and were lighting a shuck in the Hell Wagon.

22

Cuno checked all three rifles in the rack. Only two were loaded. Taking one of the loaded rifles in his left hand, he grabbed the other in his right and sprang toward the open door.

"Give me rifle!" Kong shouted behind him.

Cuno hesitated, then turned and tossed the Winchester to the Chinaman, who caught it one-handed, deftly lowered the rifle to his side, and opened the breech to check the loads himself.

It appeared that the Indian bow and arrow wasn't the only weapon the Chinaman knew his way around.

Cuno dashed outside as the wagon streaked past the jail — a large black shadow bounding off to Cuno's left behind six screaming horses tossing their heads at the diminishing gunfire.

Two horseback riders galloped out front

of the wagon while six more followed behind it. Two of them wore tin stars on their chests.

In the street before the bank, four blue-uniformed figures slumped, blood glistening in the growing morning light. The wagon guards and driver.

As the six riders approached the jailhouse from the right, Cuno bolted into the street, stopped, spread his feet, and raised the Winchester.

"Look out!" one of the deputies screamed.

Cuno fired.

He levered the rifle and fired repeatedly, watching through his powder smoke as the .44 slugs tore through tunics and dusters, punched into thighs and faces and arms, tearing away chunks of flesh and bone, spraying blood.

One slug drilled a tin star to exit out the small of the man's back, ricochet off the street, and plunk through a window of the millinery shop.

Horses reared, screamed, plunged. The riders yelled in agony, windmilling from their saddles. Terrified by the fusillade, five of the six horses shook their heads and continued forward at full gallop. The sixth, a claybank, tumbled head over heels, its own limbs entangled with those of its rider. Dust wafted as if a twister had run through town.

The wounded men were still rolling in the street when Cuno turned to peer after the wagon. For some reason, it had stopped two blocks away. Enraged exclamations rose, sounding hollow between the two rows of false-fronted buildings.

Kong could finish off the six men in the street — if there were any to finish.

Cuno sprinted forward through the gun smoke and sifting dust, the horse that had somersaulted now giving an indignant whinny and gaining its feet to his right. The saddle had fallen down its right side. Its rider lay twisted horribly in the middle of the street, bleeding from his mouth and ears.

As a final insult, the horse set one foot down in the man's gut. The man convulsed, farting and grunting loudly as air spurted from his lungs. Frightened by the man's reaction, the horse shook its head, turned uncertainly, and cantered off down an alley.

Ahead, someone shouted, "Get that fucking heap outta the goddamn street, you old bastard!"

A shotgun boomed and a man grunted. A pistol popped, the slug thwapping into solid wood planking.

"That one there's for Wade!" a familiar

286

voice shouted from the same area.

Another man cursed. *"The old bastard's got a shotgun!"*

As if in reply, the voice of Serenity Parker roared, "And here's another one fer ole Wade!"

Ka-boooom!

Running along the boardwalk, Cuno was thirty feet from the wagon when the driver jerked back in his seat, then fell heavily down the vehicle's left side. He smacked the iron-shod wheel with a muffled thud, painting the rim bright red, and hit the street on his side.

Cuno stopped and stared.

In front of the fiddle-footing six-horse hitch, Serenity Parker sat the driver's box of Cuno's big Murphy freight wagon. The oldster had pulled the wagon into the path of the Hell Wagon, the Murphy's box directly in front of the horses. The wizened graybeard had broken his double-barreled Greener open and was flipping out the spent wads.

"Old man, get down!" Cuno shouted as the two lead riders swung their horses around, heading back toward the Hell Wagon.

Cuno bolted forward, but stopped when he heard the squawk of iron hinges. He turned to the wagon.

The armored side door swung open and two men bolted out — one a handsome, dark-haired cuss in a black frock and black hat. The other was a mean-looking hombre with a scruffy beard, milky eye, and a hummingbird tattooed on his cheek. Behind them Cuno saw Glory crouched in a corner, head in her arms, body wracked with sobs.

Seeing Cuno, the handsome gent crouched and raised his well-oiled revolver. The slug plinked into a window behind Cuno.

Cuno brought the Winchester to bear and fired three quick rounds, one taking the handsome gent through his chest, the other burning across the temple of the bearded, one-eyed man. As both men went down screaming, Cuno ejected the smoking shell and looked beyond the Murphy.

The two lead riders galloped toward him, triggering pistols at Serenity crouched in the box with his shotgun. The slugs chewed the wood in the seat and barked off the steel rail above the dashboard.

Cuno fired three quick shots over Serenity's head. One of the riders flew off his horse while the other reined up, trying to get a bead on Cuno.

The freighter ran around the four braying

mules hitched to the Murphy. Serenity was muttering curses under his breath as he thumbed fresh wads into the Greener, oblivious to the gunshots.

"Old man, I'm not gonna tell you again!"

Cuno dove behind a stock trough as two slugs kicked up dust before him and another shattered the window of the tonsorial parlor to his left. He snaked his own rifle around the stock trough, planted a bead on the horseback rider, and fired.

The slug punched through the man's right thigh near the hip. He was a half-breed with light-red skin and long, dark-brown hair under a shabby bowler hat decorated with a single silver concho. Wearing two shoulder holsters over a beaded vest, he grimaced, showing a few tobacco-brown teeth, then jerked his reins taut as the horse skitter-stepped and nickered.

Cuno strode into the street. He triggered the Winchester.

It clicked empty.

The half-breed turned toward him on his agitated horse. Smiling and whooping, he loosed a shot. It ground into an awning post. Cuno threw away the rifle, palmed his .45, crouched, and fired.

Pop, pop, pop!

Three bloody welts appeared in the half-breed's shoulder, neck, and right cheek.

The horse screamed and reared.

The half-breed turned a somersault and hit the ground on his head, his neck snapping audibly.

The horse raced away.

To Cuno's right, a pistol spoke and a shotgun boomed twice. He ignored it as he peered through the horse's dust, toward the other side of the street. The first lead rider he'd shot was climbing to his feet, hatless, lips stretched back from his teeth. He glanced at Cuno, then bolted toward a stock trough.

Cuno's Colt leapt and barked three times, wafting smoke.

The man groaned as he fell behind the stock trough.

Quickly reloading, Cuno strode toward the other side of the street, replacing the .45 cartridges by rote, staring at the stock trough. He thumbed in the sixth cartridge, flipped the loading gate closed, and peered over the trough.

Behind it, the man lay with his head resting against the boardwalk. He appeared the oldest man of the bunch, with a pitted, deep-lined face and sandy hair streaked with gray. His upper lip was knife-scarred. His chest rose and fell sharply. Blood puddled his belly and both shoulders.

He winced and gazed sharply up at Cuno. "I'm Ned Crockett. Who the fuck're you?"

"Cuno Massey."

Crockett spat a stream of blood to one side.

"You're right handy with a .45." His chin dropped. He rolled to his right shoulder and lay still.

Cuno saw someone move to his right. He turned to see the man he'd wounded stumbling into an alley, disappearing between two unpainted buildings.

Farther down the street, several shots cracked.

A man stumbled toward Cuno, fifty yards away. A big black man with a black beard and clad all in black. He was breathing hard, wheezing. Kong strode after him, limping slightly, blood showing on his right thigh.

The Chinaman raised his Winchester and fired, quickly ejected the spent shell.

The black man jerked with a start, fell to a knee. He lowered his head. Wincing, he looked behind, snaked a revolver across his body to shoot at Kong.

Kong fired the Winchester. The black man's head jerked sharply, blood and brains spraying out the hole above his right ear.

The black man sagged to the street, legs kicking wildly.

"That's Cannady!"

Cuno turned sharply right. Serenity Parker lay beneath the Murphy wagon, staring out between the two rear wheels, holding his smoking shotgun in both hands. His face was crimson behind his tangled, gray beard. He nodded as he gazed into the alley.

"Get the son of a bitch! I done gave him about twelve buckshot in his right shoulder!"

Cuno turned toward the alley mouth.

Cannady.

He remembered Serenity mentioning the man had a hummingbird tattoo on his cheek.

"I'll fetch him."

Holding his .45 down by his right thigh, Cuno strode into the alley. Walking like a drunk, dragging his toes, Cannady stumbled off into the rocks and brush beyond town. The top of his right shoulder was peppered with a dozen bloody welts.

Twenty feet behind Cannady, Cuno called the man's name. Cannady swung heavily, bringing his Remington up. Cuno's slug punched through Cannady's upper right arm.

Cannady dropped the gun and grabbed

the arm, thick red blood seeping through his fingers. He cursed loudly and continued stumbling forward. He took three steps, dropped to a knee, and peered over his left shoulder, squinting his white eye.

"Fuck you, ye goddamn, copper-riveted bastard!"

Cannady rolled onto his butt and pushed himself backward with his heels, carving a broad furrow in the dust. His good eye stared, bright with rage and terror, at Cuno. The hummingbird on his cheek had turned spruce green against the crimson of his sweaty dirt-streaked face.

He'd only slid a few feet before he stopped, exhausted, chest heaving.

Cuno stopped before him, stared down at him. He held his pistol down by his thigh. "I'm Wade Scanlon's partner."

Cannady's voice rose with defiance. "That name don't mean *shit* to me!"

Cuno raised the revolver, canted the barrel toward Cannady's right knee. He fired. The bullet cracked through the knob of the knee, the smoking hole in his denims filling with blood.

Cannady clutched the ruined bone, throwing his head back and scrunching up his face. He howled.

"Does that refresh your memory?"

Cannady howled again.

Cuno drilled a round through Cannady's other knee.

Cannady threw his head back and set both hands on the ground, the cords and tendons standing out in his neck as he arched his back and screamed like a wounded coyote.

Cuno watched the man writhe on the ground.

Cannady's eyes shunted to Cuno's — filled with misery and beseeching. Tears streaked his beard. "You . . . you the reason my brother and the others" — he winced, panting — "ain't caught up to us?"

"I killed your brother and the others deader'n hell."

Cannady winced again and swallowed hard, his good eye acquiring a dark, hopeless cast. "Well, what're ya waiting fer? Finish me, you bastard!"

Cuno holstered the .45. "I'm gonna sleep well nights, thinkin' about you workin' the prison rock quarries with those two ruined knees and that shattered arm."

Cannady's grunts and snarls turned to sobs as he glanced at his two bloody knees.

Cuno smiled, turned, and walked back toward Serenity standing in the middle of the street, holding his broken-open shotgun under one arm, like a bird hunter. Serenity was grinning broadly through his thick, gray beard, pale-gray eyes glistening in the climbing morning sun.

Cuno glanced at the big Murphy freighter sitting before the Hell Wagon. "Nice timing, old-timer."

"Told ye I was good fer somethin'." Serenity nodded at Cannady. "You really just gonna leave him like that?"

"Why not?"

Serenity cackled and shook his head as Cuno brushed past him, heading toward where Kong lay in the street near the dead black man. Li Mei, dressed in a black robe, was kneeling beside her father. Cuno knelt near Kong's right elbow, peered at the blood dappling the man's blue wool shirt just above his left hip.

"It's just a graze," the girl told Cuno.

Kong's almond-shaped eyes slitted devilishly as he glanced at the black man lying nearby with his brains blown out. "Good shooting, huh?"

Cuno allowed himself a smile. "Not bad." Peering down the street, he saw several shop owners and the doctor moving amongst the dead men before the bank, inspecting each body for life.

Cuno whistled to catch the sawbones's attention, then pointed down at Kong.

"It's just a scratch," Kong said. "Li Mei can tend . . ." His voice trailed off as his gaze strayed to something behind Cuno.

Cuno turned a glance over his right shoulder. Glory stood near the Hell Wagon. She wore a green wool traveling skirt, a frilly white blouse, and a broad-brimmed, green felt hat. A pearl-gripped, .36-caliber pistol jutted from the soft leather holster on her right hip.

She regarded him shame-faced, blond hair sifting about her cheeks. Tears glistened in her blue eyes.

Cuno straightened, facing her. "The outlaw girl."

"It wasn't my fault," she pouted. "Case offered me four thousand dollars and safe passage to Mexico City."

"For what?"

She brushed her cheek with her hand. "Findin' out when the Hell Wagon was due."

"How'd you manage that?"

Glory lifted a shoulder. A tear rolled down her cheek. "The mine manager . . ."

Cuno nodded and chuckled. "A customer."

Glory scrunched her eyes with halfhearted defiance. "I didn't do anything any other girl wouldn't have done in the same position. I'm tired of spreadin' my legs for a livin'."

"You prefer breakin' rock in the federal pen like Cannady?" Cuno grabbed her arm, pulled her along as he moved to one of the dead renegade's horses standing with its reins dangling.

"What're you doin'?" Taking quick, mincing steps along beside him, Glory tried to pry his thick fingers off her arm. "That hurts!"

"Be grateful I don't spank your bare bottom with a saddle quirt. Or throw you to the law."

He threw her onto the saddle, her skirt flying awry, then flipped the reins at her. "Get outta here!"

"I don't have nowhere to go!"

"Knowing you, you'll find a place."

"I didn't wanna do it, Cuno. I didn't have a choice."

He glared up at her. "None of us does anything we don't wanna do, Glory. We all have a choice." He slapped the horse's rump. The buckskin reared, lunged off its hind hooves, and galloped west. After nearly falling off, the girl slumped forward, clutching the saddle horn, her hair bouncing on her shoulders.

The horse streaked past an oncoming ore

297

wagon, the driver craning his neck to follow the horse and its pretty, sobbing rider with his eyes. The buckskin crested a distant grade and disappeared down the other side.

Cuno cursed and climbed into the Murphy's driver's box.

"Hey, where you goin'?" Serenity called.

Cuno released the brake and whipped the horses around the Hell Wagon, heading east along Main.

"I'm gonna off-load these supplies. Then I'm headin' for a saloon." Glancing over his left shoulder, Cuno added, "I'll be there awhile!"

Serenity stared after him, squinting into the dust. The old man snorted and bit off a hunk from the tobacco braid in his right hand. "Now you're talkin'!"

ABOUT THE AUTHOR

Peter Brandvold was born and raised in North Dakota. He currently resides in Colorado. His website is www.peterbrand vold.com. You can drop him an e-mail at pgbrandvold@msn.com.

The employees of Thorndike Press hope you have enjoyed this Large Print book. All our Thorndike and Wheeler Large Print titles are designed for easy reading, and all our books are made to last. Other Thorndike Press Large Print books are available at your library, through selected bookstores, or directly from us.

For information about titles, please call:
(800) 223-1244

or visit our Web site at:
http://gale.cengage.com/thorndike

To share your comments, please write:
Publisher
Thorndike Press
295 Kennedy Memorial Drive
Waterville, ME 04901